HEARTS *of* AMISH COUNTRY™

Love's SIMPLE DUTY

Mary Alford

Annie's®

AnniesFiction.com

Library of Congress-in-Publication Data
Love's Simple Duty / by Mary Alford
p. cm.
I. Title
                        2019936979

AnniesFiction.com
(800) 282-6643
Hearts of Amish Country™
Series Creator: Shari Lohner
Series Editor: Jane Haertel

10 11 12 13 14 | Printed in China | 9 8 7 6 5 4 3 2 1

1

"**M**amm!"

The back door of Deborah Albrecht's fabric shop flew open and Deborah shot to her feet, the white organdy apron she'd been working on for her friend Faith's upcoming wedding all but forgotten.

Her son, Thad, burst in and skidded to a stop in front of her, eyes wide and face pale as a freshly washed sheet.

"*Was iss letz*?" Deborah asked with her heart in her throat. Kneeling in front of the boy, she clasped his shoulders. "Thad, tell me what is wrong."

"Nothing!" he exclaimed, his voice higher than usual. Thad's innocent face scrunched up in a mutinous expression she rarely saw. He avoided her gaze, confirming that he wasn't telling the truth. As far as she knew, Thad had never lied to her before.

Deborah glanced through the open back door at the woods beyond her shop. She normally closed the shop around four to give herself time to go home and take care of the chores around the *Haus*. But today, she'd wanted to finish up the last apron for Faith's wedding, so she'd closed around lunchtime.

A frown creased her brow. "Where is David? I thought you two were playing together." David Zook had been Thad's best friend since the two boys were old enough to walk.

"His Mamm came to get him for dinner, so I went to explore in the woods," Thad mumbled, still without meeting her gaze.

"But where is your coat?"

Tears welled in the boy's eyes, his bottom lip trembling. "I don't know. I guess I left it in the woods."

Seeing her son's tears broke her heart. This past year had been a hard one for them both without Peter, but it was devastating for a boy of eight, losing his *Daed* in such a tragic way.

She gathered him close and gently brushed aside his tears. "Don't cry, my *Boppli*. Everything will be fine. I am sure we can find your coat on our way home." The tremors running through his little body scared her more than anything. Thad was fearless most days.

"*Come*, it is getting late. We can find the coat and be home before dark if we hurry." She placed a kiss on his forehead, then rose to her feet and carefully placed the apron on her work table.

Deborah hurried to lock the front door, then removed her black woolen cloak from the peg by the door. Once she tied it in place, she placed her black traveling bonnet over her white *Kapp*.

Outside, dark skies threatened snow. At this time of the year, with winter's approach, evening came quickly in the San Luis Valley of Colorado, which was tucked between the Sangre de Cristo and the San Juan Mountains.

A freezing wind whipped through the shop, sending a shiver down Deborah's spine. She took Thad's hand and stepped out into the twilight. "We must hurry. Lucy is arriving later tonight and I want to make sure everything is ready for her."

When Deborah first received the letter from a young Amish woman from Canada by the name of Lucy Miller, it surprised her to learn she'd gotten Deborah's name from a kindly old couple who'd moved away. Lucy had said the family thought highly of Deborah and suggested Lucy contact her for help.

In her letter, Lucy asked if she could stay with Deborah for a few weeks until her brother and his wife were able to join her in the San

Luis Valley, where they planned to buy a place of their own and make the community their home.

Honored, Deborah had promptly written Lucy back, agreeing to the proposal. As the young woman's arrival date drew nearer, Deborah found herself looking forward to having another grown-up in the Haus. She missed talking to Peter so much. Not a minute passed when she didn't think of something she wanted to share with him, only to remember the painful truth that she couldn't.

Thad clutched her hand tightly as they stepped from the back porch, gluing himself to her side much as he had when he was a toddler. At eight, Thad's emotions shifted between childhood and adolescence. When his friends were around, he didn't like affection from his Mamm, but when it was just the two of them, he'd occasionally let her cuddle him.

As they approached the woods, Thad hung back. Normally, he'd run ahead, examining whatever caught his eye.

"Hurry, Thad. It's cold, and it will be dark soon, and we still need to find your coat before we start home." As she moved toward the woods once more, Thad stopped dead without warning. When she pivoted to look at him, fresh tears shimmered in his eyes.

"What is it, Thad?" Her concern grew. "Just tell me."

"I don't want to go through the woods. Can we take the long way home? Please, Mamm," Thad pleaded, his sweet face turned up to hers.

In an instant, she forgot all about the walk home. The growing darkness. Her upcoming guest. Her son was hurting, and she didn't understand why. Kneeling next to him, she tilted up his chin to study his innocent face. "Did something happen earlier while you were playing in the woods?"

He shook free of her grasp, tears streaming down his face. "*Nay*! Nothing happened. I just want to take the long way this time. Can we?"

Though she owned a horse and buggy, Deborah chose to walk to work most days because it was a short distance from their home when they traveled through the woods behind her shop. Having to pass the cluster of Amish stores then circling down through the valley made the journey twice as long. It would be well after dark before they arrived home, and she still wanted to check Lucy's room one final time. But none of that mattered when her son needed her.

She brushed back his hair then gently wiped his tears. "Just this one time."

While Thad visibly relaxed, he didn't let go of her hand, almost as if he needed the comfort of his Mamm's touch. Together, they rounded the corner of her shop and headed to the front of the small group of Amish businesses scattered around the valley.

Thad's teeth chattered from the cold. Deborah slipped off her cloak and tied it around his shoulders. "Better?" she asked, and he nodded.

Several lights still shown in the businesses around the valley. "Troyer's Store is open," Deborah said, smiling down at Thad. "Let's stop by and see if they have something you can wear home. I can look for your Daed's coat tomorrow. I know you love to wear it, but it's too big. It's time to buy you a new one anyway."

Thad smiled for the first time and her heart melted at the sight of it. Often, it shocked her how much her son resembled Peter. The same dark hair. The same soulful brown eyes that always appeared so serious. The boy was a constant reminder of the man she'd loved with all her heart. She would always have a piece of Peter in Thad.

They neared the small diner run by the family of Deborah's good friend, Gertie Wyse. Several years before, Gertie's Mamm and Daed had turned the diner over to Gertie and her *Mann*, Samuel, much to Gertie's delight. Deborah and Gertie had been friends since their school days, sharing so many dreams growing up. They'd gone through their *Rumspringa* together, joined the church, and married around the same time.

"Want to stop in and say hello to Gertie and Samuel first?" she asked. Thad loved visiting the diner because Gertie spoiled him with little treats.

"*Ja*, can we?" Thad's face lit up, his earlier cares gone for the moment.

"We can." Happy to see him acting like his old self again, she tousled his hair and led him into the warmth of the diner.

The bell above the door jingled their arrival. Gertie glanced up from stirring something in the kitchen and spotted Deborah and Thad. Smiling, she wiped her hands on a towel and hurried from behind the counter. Hugging Deborah tight, she patted Thad's head affectionately.

Tonight, the cold and impending snow kept most would-be diners away. Not even Gertie's warm home cooking could draw them out.

"This is a lovely surprise. What brings you two out at this time of the evening?" Gertie asked, then peered out at the darkening skies.

Gertie glanced Thad's way, concern furrowing her brow. The boy still hung onto Deborah's hand, a reminder that things were not quite back to normal yet.

"We need to buy a new coat for Thad. Troyer's is still open, so we'd best hurry along. I just wanted to pop in and say hello."

"I see." Gertie was clearly curious.

"I'll tell you later," Deborah whispered.

Gertie nodded.

So far, *Gött* had not blessed Gertie and Samuel with children of their own, but Gertie remained prayerful.

"Would you two like some supper after you finish your shopping? With the weather moving in, it doesn't look like we're going to be busy tonight so we plan to close up early. We could give you a ride home afterward. It would be nice to spend some time together. We're all so busy these days." Gertie threw up her hands. It seemed the only time they got to visit was at the biweekly Sunday church service and meal.

Though Deborah wanted to accept, money was tight and she hesitated. It took all her shop earnings, along with the dresses she sewed in her spare time, to keep a roof over their heads. Still, sharing a meal with friends might be just the thing to help Thad forget whatever had spooked him. She'd put her faith in Gött to provide for their needs.

Smiling, she nodded. "Ja, that would be nice."

"*Gut*, because I made friendship soup and fresh bread for dinner, and it would be a shame to let it go to waste."

Deborah's stomach rumbled as tantalizing aromas wafted in from the kitchen. "That sounds wonderful for a chilly evening such as this. We will be right back." With a quick wave, she and Thad hurried out the door, her thoughts a million miles away.

She'd barely cleared the door when she collided with someone walking past the diner. Two strong hands reached out to steady her.

"I'm sorry. I didn't see you coming out." His deep voice swept over her and she quickly stepped back. His hands dropped to his sides.

Judging by his jeans and leather jacket, he was *Englisch*. He was tall, with broad shoulders and dark blond hair. Deborah tipped her head back to peer into kind, clear blue eyes. *He's so handsome.* The thought popped into her head involuntarily.

Color slipped into her cheeks. Embarrassed by her reaction, she pulled her gaze away. "It's okay. I wasn't watching where I was going," she said in English.

"It's no problem. Eben Graber." His smile was genuine. He stuck his hand out and she stared at it. The name sounded Amish. Perhaps she was wrong.

"Deborah Albrecht." She shook his hand. His grasp was firm, and a jolt of awareness swept from their joined hands. Did he feel it too?

Nothing but curiosity showed on his attractive face. She withdrew her hand, and his smile slipped a little.

"It's nice to meet you, Deborah." He glanced down at Thad. "And who is this?"

Deborah drew the boy closer in a protective gesture. "This is my son, Thad."

"Nice to meet you, too, Thad," Eben said, grinning down at him.

Was he a simple traveler passing through the area? The community did see its share of visitors, but usually in the summer months. She noticed he held something in his hand. Right away, Deborah recognized it. Thad's coat.

He caught her staring at it. "I found this in the woods earlier. Does it belong to you?" he asked, correctly interpreting her surprise. "Though it seems a little big for you yet," he said to Thad.

"It's Thad's. Thank you for retrieving it."

He handed her the coat. "You're welcome."

Suddenly not wanting the conversation to end, she asked, "Are you having dinner here?"

"Oh—yes. I'm on my way in now." She glanced past him at the single car parked in front of the diner. His? If so, then of course she'd been right. He was Englisch.

"Well, enjoy your dinner," she murmured and turned on her heel, heading for Troyer's with Thad tucked close to her skirt. Something about this man's sudden appearance left her feeling unsettled. She needed space to clear her head. Even though she now had Thad's coat, she still needed to buy him one that fit before having dinner with Gertie and Samuel.

When she reached the front of the store, Deborah turned to look at Eben, unable to stop herself. His smile disappeared. He was watching them.

Eben waited until Deborah and the boy went inside, then grabbed his cell phone and turned away. "I've made contact. What do you want me to do?" he asked, scanning the surrounding countryside for the trouble he knew was coming.

"Until Lucy's in place, don't let them out of your sight for a minute." Unease raced up Eben's spine at his commander's words. "I have bad news. They released Benson from prison last night and no one bothered to let us know." The annoyance in Brian Anderson's tone was clear.

"You're kidding." Eben couldn't believe what he'd just heard.

"I wish I was. You know how dangerous this guy is. We have every reason to believe he may be coming after Deborah Albrecht and her son. Keep your eyes open and call me immediately if anything jumps out."

"I will," Eben promised and ended the call, putting the phone away. The news of Benson's early release troubled him.

In addition to money laundering, the FBI believed Victor Benson had murdered Deborah's husband, Peter, one of the Amish men who worked for him, because of something Peter had witnessed.

Eben's team had been quietly investigating the Amish man's death when Benson's business partner, Ed Zachary, turned him in for tax evasion and Benson had been incarcerated. Now Benson was out of prison, and they still lacked the evidence to put him away for the murder.

Based on a tip provided by Benson's cellmate who worked as an FBI informant, Eben believed there was another reason to be concerned. In addition to coming after Deborah and Thad, Benson had found out Ed Zachary had changed his name to Henry Yoder and was passing himself off as an Amish man living in the San Luis Valley community.

Benson likely wanted revenge on the former business partner who had gotten him imprisoned.

In preparation for infiltrating the community, Eben's fellow agent, Lucy Miller, had sent a letter to Deborah the week before asking for a place to stay. Lucy, posing as an Amish woman from Milverton, Canada, would be in place later that night. Until then, Eben couldn't afford to let Deborah or the boy out of his sight for a second, especially with Benson on the loose.

Eben glanced around the small town, hating the deceit necessary to maintain his cover story. The Amish people were simple. Honest. Peace loving. His presence threatened all of those things.

At one time, these could have been his people. He had been raised plain, calling the Amish community in Charlotte County, Virginia, home for seventeen years. Then, soon after Eben's birthday, his father suddenly uprooted the family and moved them away. A devastated Eben had been forced to leave his beloved *Grossdaddi* and *Grossmammi*. He hadn't found out until much later the true reason why his father left the community.

Caleb had gone to work for an Englischer to support his family. The man insisted he learn to drive a vehicle, giving him a car to perform his job of driving his employer around to doctor's appointments and other needs, with the bishop's permission. But Caleb had taken advantage of the situation and, to earn extra money, used the vehicle as an unsanctioned taxi for the Amish people. When the bishop discovered Caleb's deceit, Caleb was brought before the bishop and elders. Asked to confess his sin and give up his job, Caleb let his pride get in the way and ended up excommunicated.

Out of respect for his father, Eben had never been baptized or joined the church, a decision he had often debated within himself. He'd made a life in the Englisch world, but the separation from his grandparents had been the hardest part of leaving the community. He'd made it a point to go home whenever possible to visit them until they passed. He carried the ache of their loss with him always.

The memories were too painful, and he shoved the past back where it belonged. Reliving it served no purpose. "That which is done cannot be undone," his Grossdaddi always said.

Eben spotted Deborah watching him from the porch of the store, a worried frown marring her pretty face. He'd made her uncomfortable, which was not his intention. Eben hadn't been sure what to expect when they met, yet from the moment he'd looked into those haunted green eyes, he felt a stirring down deep inside like nothing he'd experienced before.

She was lovely. Wisps of golden hair peeked out from beneath her traveling bonnet. The black dress and cloak accentuating unadorned, flawless skin. Old longings for the life that should have been his boiled to the surface. He'd dreamed of having a *Fraa* like her to share his life one day and *Kinner* around his table.

Regret seared his heart. He glanced away from Deborah's worried gaze and shook his head. Standing here like this called dangerous attention to himself.

When he'd spotted Thad running from the woods behind Deborah's fabric shop while doing surveillance around the community, he'd known something was wrong. The look of terror on the boy's face had sent Eben springing into action. He'd waited until the boy was safely inside before investigating. That's when he found the coat shoved behind a tree at the entrance to the woods. Before he could check further, Deborah had emerged from the house with her son. He'd had no choice but to follow them while keeping a careful distance.

Eben saw Deborah and the boy leaving the store. He straightened and tried to appear less conspicuous.

She hesitated when she saw him standing in the same place where she'd left him. Slowly, she approached, her expression wary. "Do you need directions?" she asked politely.

He forced a smile. "Actually I was wondering if you and Thad were going inside the diner."

Something flashed in her eyes. He'd made her uncomfortable again. Eben, of all people, should know better. He could almost see the debate going on inside her before she slowly smiled, catching him off guard. It lit up her face and eased some of the sadness etched around her pretty eyes.

Glancing down at the boy, she said, "We are. My friend Gertie has soup and bread waiting on us. And probably some treats for Thad."

He'd been ordered to watch her, but Eben found himself wanting to get to know her better too. He couldn't imagine how difficult this past year must have been for her, raising the boy alone. Something about her drew him in. Perhaps because she reminded him of the life he'd once loved. The love he'd hoped for.

"Maybe I could join you." He stopped, realizing he'd made another foolish mistake. She didn't know him. "I'm sorry. I will sit at a different table, of course."

Deborah opened the door and ushered her son into the restaurant. "You are free to sit wherever you would like, Eben Graber." At first, he thought she rebuked him for being so forward until he caught a glint of humor shimmering in her eyes.

"Thank you," he managed, his voice unsteady. He followed her into the small diner that appeared typical of most any found among the plain communities. A dozen or more Amish handcrafted tables filled the small dining area. Simple red-and-white gingham tablecloths covered them. A single red flower rested in a glass vase on each. The place's homey feel would welcome both its Amish patrons and the occasional Englisch traveler.

A man and woman around Deborah's age worked behind the counter. There were no other diners in the establishment.

Deborah went up to the counter where the woman stood, not quite able to hide her shock at seeing him walk in with them. Noticing her friend's surprise, Deborah faced him. "Gertie, this is Eben Graber, a visitor to our community."

Her introduction took him aback, but the woman behind the counter didn't seem to think anything of it. "Welcome, Eben." She came around the counter and extended her hand. He shook it. "Will you be having the same as these two?"

Eben peered from the woman to Deborah, who continued to watch him with those mesmerizing eyes as if trying to understand his sudden appearance in her town.

"Um, yes. If it's no trouble," he added while trying to recall what Deborah told him they were having. He needed to get a grip. Normally, he possessed more control over his emotions than this. Something about Deborah had rattled him to his core.

She pulled out a chair and sat at one of the tables. The boy followed. Not sure what to do, he waited for her to decide. "Won't you join us? It's the least I can do to thank you for returning Thad's coat. It has special meaning for him."

Eben slid out a chair across from her, curious. "Why is that?"

Her smile faded, sadness replacing it. "It belonged to Thad's father. He passed away last year."

"I'm so sorry." Eben knew all too well what happened to Peter Albrecht. Though it had been officially ruled an accident, the fall from the roof was anything but. They only needed the proof to convict Benson of the crime.

Eben couldn't imagine how difficult the loss of his father must be for Thad. Although Caleb had brought shame on his family, he was a crucial part of Eben's life. Even today, they spent time together whenever possible.

When the silence between them drew on, and he couldn't think of anything to say to change that, Deborah cleared her throat and asked, "What brings you to our community, Eben Graber?" He suspected she enjoyed teasing him by using his full name, yet he didn't mind.

"I recently bought the Glick place outside of town. I want to fix it up and make it a workable farm again. But my trade is in construction. I'm a good craftsman and a hard worker," Eben said, sticking with his cover story.

Though her expression was puzzled, Deborah was too polite to ask why an Englischer would want to take up residence among the Amish.

When he'd been told he'd stay at a former Amish homestead, Eben understood what that meant. No electricity, none of the modern conveniences he'd grown accustomed to as an adult.

Gertie brought their meals to the table. "My husband and I could use some carpentry help," she said, overhearing their discussion. "We are expanding the diner soon." She turned back to the kitchen. "Samuel, this man is a carpenter."

Samuel popped his head out. He was a giant of a man with a boyish smile. "That so?"

Eben hadn't expected this conversation and he swallowed before answering. "Yes, it is." He'd worked alongside his Grossdaddi repairing things around the place until his grandparents' passing. His Grossdaddi taught him the value of hard work and doing things right the first time. The times he spent on their farm were some of Eben's favorite memories.

Samuel came out of the kitchen, wiping his hands. "The job would only be part-time, but I could use the extra help. How soon could you start?"

Surprised he'd gotten a job offer without really looking for one, Eben glanced from Samuel to the woman seated across from him. She waited for his answer as well.

The offer might prove to be a blessing in disguise. Being part-time he'd still be able to search for Benson, plus he'd be close to Deborah's work as well as Thad's school. He could keep a watchful eye out for them during the day.

"In a few days, if that's okay. I need to get settled into the house first."

Samuel nodded and stuck out his hand. "Ja, that is okay. You need the chance to make it your home. You will come find me when you are ready?"

"I will," Eben assured him, then shook Samuel's hand. "*Denki*," he added without thinking about it. For the first time in longer than he remembered, probably since his grandparents' deaths, Eben felt as if he belonged somewhere. Was it just a coincidence that it was here, among the Amish people his father had left behind?

2

Deborah couldn't remember the last time a simple meal of friend-ship soup—rich broth brimming with ground beef, onions, lentils, and barley—had tasted so *gut*. She had to admit it was the man seated across the table who made the meal a particularly delicious one. Some of the grief encasing her heart slipped away. She found herself actu-ally smiling and laughing at his jokes, relishing his company.

When had she become so foolish? It was just nice to share a meal with others, she told herself. She had enough worries and complications in her life without needlessly adding another. What had happened with Thad earlier still weighed heavy in her thoughts. Growing up in the wide-open country of Colorado, Thad had fished alongside his father for years. He feared very little, yet something had spooked him.

The battery-operated diner lights kept the darkness outside at bay. Deborah glanced at the clock on the wall. She'd had no idea it was so late. Lucy would arrive any moment, and they still had a long walk home. Regret flooded her heart. "Thad, we must say goodbye to Mr. Graber. It's time for us to leave."

"Aw, Mamm, do we have to?" Thad protested. She was not the only one who already liked Eben.

"Ja, we do." Gathering their bowls, Deborah carried them to the kitchen, where Gertie was briskly ladling soup. In the short period of time they'd sat and talked, the diner had experienced an influx of customers.

Placing the dishes in the sink, she faced her friend.

Gertie wiped her forehead on her apron. "You aren't leaving, are you?" she asked with regret in her tone.

"Ja, it is time. We must get home before Lucy arrives." Deborah had told her friend all about her houseguest at the Sunday service.

"I'm so sorry. I had no idea it would get this busy. Are you sure you can't wait until we close? Samuel and I can drive you home then. I hate to think of you walking so far in the dark."

Gertie had her hands full, and she and Thad had walked home many times after dark. Their community was a peaceful one. Everyone looked after each other.

"Don't worry about us. We will be fine." She took out some money to pay for their meals, but Gertie folded her arms over her chest.

"You and Thad are family. It is a blessing to feed family."

"But this is your livelihood," Deborah argued.

"Deborah Albrecht, you put that money away right now or I will tug your Kapp down over your eyes as I did when we quarreled as Kinner."

Resolving to make sure some fabric Gertie had been eyeing wound up in her friend's home soon, Deborah obeyed with a laugh. "Denki, Gertie."

"That's more like it." She glanced into the dining room where Thad seemed to hang on Eben's every word. "He's an interesting person, ain't so? Thad is getting along with him too. I expect he misses his Daed a great deal."

Eben chuckled at something Thad said, the smile lighting up his face. Eben had a serious demeanor in general, she'd noticed in the hour or so she'd known him. But in that moment he seemed carefree.

She turned and realized Gertie was watching her.

"Good night, Gertie. Denki again. Your friendship soup was

delicious as always. Your Mamm would be proud." She leaned over and gave her friend a hug.

"I hope so. I like to do justice to her recipes. Be careful going home. Here, take one of our lanterns to light your way." Gertie hurried to the back door and removed a lantern from its peg, then lit it. "Be safe now, and stay warm."

Deborah smiled. "Ja, I will." With a final wave to Samuel, she carried the lantern back to their table, where Eben rose to his feet.

"I should be on my way as well." He went to the counter, ready to pay, but Gertie refused.

"You keep your money. We are happy to have you helping us out with the diner."

He inclined his head. "That's very generous. Thank you for the opportunity." With a lift of his hand, he came over to where Deborah and Thad waited next to the door.

Taking her cloak and traveling bonnet from the wall peg, Deborah slipped them on while Eben held the lantern, his piercing gaze fixed on her face. Her fingers shook a little. What was wrong with her?

He held the door open for them. She and Thad stepped out into the inky darkness of another night settling in over the valley. The temperature grew colder with nightfall. Fat snowflakes had begun to fall from dark skies and dread wrapped itself around her like a prickly cloak. The thought of walking home in the storm was hardly a welcome one. She shivered as a gust whipped around the corner of the building, slicing through her.

Tugging Thad close, she faced Eben, hating that their time must end. "We'll be on our way now. Thank you for the company. I hope you make the farm everything you want it to be."

His lips lifted in a smile. "Denki, Deborah. I enjoyed meeting you and Thad."

Warmth filled her heart and she turned away, the tips of her ears burning. With the lantern held high, the valley with its shadows stretched out before them and she swallowed back unease.

"Deborah, wait," Eben called out after she'd only taken a few steps. She faced him again. "Let me drive you and Thad home. It's freezing out, and you have a long way to go. Much too far in these conditions."

Her eyes widened. How did he know where she lived?

Before she asked, Thad tugged at her hand. "Can we, Mamm?" His upturned face pleaded with her to say yes, the earlier incident in the woods all but forgotten in his mind, and for that she was grateful. Still, what did they really know about this man standing before them?

"Oh, I don't know. I'm sure Mr. Graber has things to do." While his company was pleasant, he did not belong to the plain life. It was best not to encourage the friendship further.

"I'm just going home," Eben assured her. "You are not keeping me from anything, and I'd be happy to drive you."

"Please, Mamm. I want to ride in a car."

Deborah felt herself giving in. This past year had been a difficult one for her son. She wanted to make him happy.

"I promise I'll drive slowly. It will be perfectly safe," Eben assured her, his gaze fixed on her face.

What was she so afraid of? It wasn't exactly proper for her to ride in the car with him, but it was cold and dark—and somehow she knew she could trust him. "Well, okay. But only if you're sure."

"I'm sure." His smile widened. "Come on, Thad, let's get you buckled inside."

"Yippee!" Thad whooped and ran to the car without waiting for Eben.

"Thad, manners!" Deborah called after him, but Eben chuckled.

"He's just excited about a new experience," he said to her. "I remember the first time I rode in a car."

She stopped walking and stared at him again. It was an unusual comment. How could any Englischer remember the first time he'd ridden in a car? She certainly didn't recall the first time she'd ridden in a buggy.

Eben unlocked the car and held the back door open so Thad could clamber inside. When the boy was safely buckled into his seat, Eben came around to the passenger side and opened the door for her. Uncertainty held her captive a moment longer, but then she blew out the lantern decisively. She'd return it to Gertie tomorrow. She sank into the soft leather seat. Eben shut the door and rounded the front of the vehicle.

He climbed in next to her, started the car, and steered it out onto the gravel street. Soon, the warmth of the car melted away the cold inside her, a welcome relief to the winter's chill they would have faced walking home.

As they drove, she became aware of the man by her side in a dozen different ways. The way his hands gripped the wheel. His strong profile. The way he smiled easily. He was the opposite of Peter in so many ways, but then, the Amish way of life was so very different.

"Everything okay?" he asked, sliding a glance her way.

She was grateful for the night's darkness, which hid the blush she felt in her cheeks. "Yes, everything is fine." She shifted in her seat to look at Thad. The boy studied the numerous buttons and lights on the car's dash with wide-eyed wonderment.

"What does the big button in the middle do?" Thad pointed to the center part of the dash.

"That controls the radio." Eben turned it on for a second.

"Whoa." Thad giggled as music came through the speakers. "Does the car go real fast?" he asked in awe.

Eben's gaze slid to Deborah. "Yes it does, but this is fast enough under these weather conditions."

"Oke." Thad's obvious disappointment didn't stop his questions. "How fast have you gone before?"

Eben shook his head. "Faster than I should have, I hate to admit." He met Thad's gaze in the rearview mirror. "A car can be dangerous if you're not paying proper attention."

Thad sank back in his seat, a look of wonder on his face as he touched the seat.

Eben turned the car onto her dirt drive without asking for directions and an uneasy feeling settled into her stomach. Again she wondered how he knew where they lived. Theirs was the only house on this side of the community other than the Glick place down from it. Something close to panic ran through her. Had getting into this car been a colossal mistake?

Eben's hands tightened on the steering wheel. "I saw you and Thad when I drove by a few days ago," he explained, as if anticipating her question. "Looks like we're neighbors."

Looking away, she chewed her bottom lip. She wanted to believe him. Worry was the opposite of faith. All she could do was put her trust in Gött and pray He would strengthen her faith.

Their place sat some distance from the road, which Deborah didn't mind. She loved the peaceful solitude of the countryside. She'd grown up in this house, learning how to cook and sew at her Mamm and Grossmammi's feet. When she and Peter wed, they'd come to live here. Deborah had loved sharing the table with three generations of family. It was so different than now, just her and Thad, unless Peter's parents visited.

The car's headlights swept across the house. As she peered through the windshield, she grasped the edge of the seat tight, her heart jumping to her throat. The front door stood ajar. *Impossible.* It was winter. Of course she'd closed that door this morning.

Eben stopped the car and shifted in his seat, frowning. "Is something wrong?" Seeing her concern, he followed her gaze.

The morning's hectic routine ran through her head. Thad had gathered eggs from the chicken coop and stopped to watch them longer than normal. By the time she'd fed the animals and milked Cinnamon, they'd had to rush through the morning meal to make sure she got Thad to school on time. As it was, the lesson was well underway when they arrived. Still, she knew she'd closed the door when they left.

She managed a nod. "Perhaps the wind blew it open." She'd always felt safe here, but after what had happened to Thad earlier . . .

Deborah opened the door to get out, but Eben touched her arm. "Let me take a quick look inside to be safe. You and Thad can wait here where it's warm."

She was not the type of woman to jump at shadows. Her Daed had taught her to be strong. She should thank Eben for the ride and send him on his way. But tonight, with the feeling inside warning her something bad was near, she thought it might be wise to proceed with caution.

The fear on her face put him on alert. The FBI expected Benson to come after the Albrechts, but Eben had hoped they'd have more time to get Lucy into place. If Benson was responsible for the open door, Eben couldn't afford to leave them alone.

"I'll be right back," he said quietly. He slipped out of the car before she had a chance to protest.

Eben stopped just outside the opened door and listened. The quiet of the countryside settled around him, until an owl hooted in the distance. The wind sang through the trees, making its own music. A sense of peacefulness pressed in as he fought back bittersweet memories.

But if Benson was close, there was nothing peaceful about what was coming.

A quick glance behind him confirmed both Deborah and Thad watched his every move. The boy's innocent face was pressed against the window, clearly visible in the moonlight. Eben slid his service weapon from his jacket pocket, trying not to let them see it. As it was, he suspected Deborah didn't fully believe his story. Switching on his flashlight with his other hand, and drawing in a deep breath, Eben inched the door open further and edged inside. Nothing stirred.

He swept the light around and surveyed a typical Amish house. A simple great room with a sofa and a couple of rockers were placed near the woodstove. A handcrafted chest in the corner of the room no doubt held blankets—which Deborah and Thad would need tonight. It would take a long time to warm up the house if the door had been open all day. The walls were bare except for a couple of quilted wall hangings above the sofa. For a moment he wondered whether they were Deborah's handiwork, or perhaps passed down from her Mamm or Grossmammi? He stepped closer to the clock on the wall. It bore a familiar Bible verse from Psalms 90:12 engraved on it. *So teach us to number our days, that we may gain a heart of wisdom.*

His Grossmammi's favorite Bible verse rendered him immobile. Poignant memories flooded his heart. He closed his eyes and could almost picture his Grossmammi hunched over her knitting, her fingers moving in perfect rhythm with the needles as she worked on a special order for one of the Englisch ladies in town. The extra money her knitting brought in helped keep the family going. When he'd gone home to clear out his grandparents' home after his Grossdaddi passed away, he'd lost count of the blankets and homemade quilts his Grossmammi had lovingly created through the years.

Drawing in a deep breath, he tried to convince himself that it was simply being back among the Amish that brought these feeling to the surface. He was just feeling nostalgic, that was all. He did his best to ignore the ache in his heart that hadn't gone away no matter how many years had passed, no matter how much his job mattered.

Moving to the kitchen, he saw a large wooden table with benches on either side, then a cast iron wood cookstove, the centerpiece of the room. The big country kitchen with cabinets painted seafoam green, off-white Formica countertops, and a pitted porcelain sink like so many others. The whole room was spotless and uncluttered. An old-fashioned percolator coffeepot sat disassembled and upside down in a dish drainer. A Dutch oven rested atop the stove.

Bitter cold seeped through his jacket, reminding him why he was there. A thorough search of the rest of the house, which consisted of three bedrooms and a small bathroom, revealed the house was empty. Nothing appeared out of place. Was the open door just the result of the wind? His gut told him differently. He'd have her do an inventory of her belongings. If Benson had searched their home, he wanted something, though Eben couldn't imagine what.

In the kitchen, he took the lantern from the table and lit it, carrying it into the great room. Using paper for kindling, which he found neatly folded along with a book of matches in a container by the stove, he loaded it into the chamber, then struck a match.

When the paper caught, then the wood, he tucked the weapon back inside his pocket, then turned off the flashlight and went outside. Deborah scrambled from the car and hurried to meet him.

"Is there a problem?" she asked in a tight voice, her eyes raking his face.

He didn't want to worry her needlessly. "Everything appears fine. I'm guessing a gust of wind caught it just right. Why don't you take a look around and see if anything is missing, just to be on the safe side?"

"You think someone came into my home?" The panic in her eyes was real, making him wonder if something more might be responsible for it. He thought about the incident in the woods earlier with Thad.

"I'm not saying that," he quickly assured her. "But you are a little way from the rest of the community. Someone might see the house empty all day and think it an easy target. Do you normally leave your door unlocked while you're away?"

Eben knew the answer already. The Amish rarely locked their doors. It wasn't that locks went against the *Ordnung* in any way. It was simply that most didn't see the need.

Deborah searched his face, still not convinced he told her the truth. "This is a peaceful community."

Eben made a mental note to try to convince her otherwise. With Benson roaming free, he couldn't afford to let her take unnecessary risks.

Thad hopped out of the back seat and ran over to his mother, listening to their exchange.

Dragging her gaze from Eben's, Deborah clasped her son's hand. "Time to go inside, Thad. Lucy will be here soon." She turned on her heel and hurried up the steps with the boy. Eben followed her inside. Deborah lit additional lanterns around the house, then began opening drawers and cabinets, checking for anything out of place.

The woodstove gave the home a warm, cheery glow. Eben recalled all the times in the past when he'd sat in front of his grandparents' stove, listening while his Grossdaddi read from the Bible.

"There is nothing missing," Deborah told him, but the worry lines around her mouth and eyes didn't go away.

After a struggle to find something to say to fill the void between them failed, he headed for the door, not sure what else to do. He'd park down at the end of her drive. It was close enough to keep an eye on the place until Lucy arrived, but hopefully far enough that she wouldn't notice he was there.

"Would you like some *Kaffe* before you head out?" she asked, taking him by surprise. "I don't usually have coffee in the evenings, but with our guest coming soon, I thought she might appreciate something warm to drink after a long day of traveling." Her evasive manner made him wonder if she didn't want to be alone.

"That would be nice." He accepted her offer willingly and followed her into the kitchen, watching as she prepared the coffee in the percolator on top of the stove. "You have a visitor coming this evening?" he asked. After all, he wasn't supposed to know about Lucy's existence.

"Yes, a young Amish woman from Canada will be staying with us awhile."

Eben feigned surprise. "That sounds interesting. I've never been to Canada before," he said, making polite conversation. Neither had Lucy, but she'd spent the week reading about the Amish community in Milverton.

His gaze held Deborah's for a moment. He watched her draw in a breath. He'd give anything to understand the meaning behind that look.

While the coffee brewed, Eben roamed into the great room where Thad sat on the floor near the fire reading a book. Quizzing the child about what had happened in the woods earlier could be tricky, but he needed to know if Thad saw anything suspicious.

He slipped into one of the rockers close to the fire. "The woods behind your Mamm's shop must be a fun place to play."

Thad didn't meet his gaze. His mouth tightened.

"I went there earlier. That's how I found your coat. You must have left in a hurry. Did something happen?"

Thad gave a tiny shake of his head, still focusing on his book.

Deborah brought coffee over to him, and he accepted it with a smile. "Thank you." Their hands touched briefly. A spark of electricity shot up from the contact spot. She quickly pulled her hand free and walked across the room to take the vacant rocker.

For most of Eben's adult life, his world had revolved around the job, the past and its failures always standing in his way of forming any lasting relationships. Now, the emptiness of his life seemed to taunt him.

"I'm sorry about your husband," he said to fill the void, but he meant it.

"He was a good man." Her gaze drifted to her son.

The noise of an approaching car saved him. Lucy. The FBI had arranged for a ride for her to make her story believable.

Deborah rose to her feet and started for the door while Thad scrambled after her, then Eben. He'd have to find a way to let Lucy know about the incident with the door.

Lucy stepped out of the car, wearing full Amish dress in the dark-blue color of the district in Canada. She seemed perfectly at ease in the clothing. But he'd worked with her before, and Lucy had proven herself more than capable in any situation.

When Lucy spotted him, she somehow kept her surprise hidden. Eben's place was supposed to be strictly behind the scenes.

His partner stepped forward and extended her hand to Deborah. "My name is Lucy Miller. Are you Deborah Albrecht?"

Deborah clasped the younger woman's hand. "Ja, I am happy to meet you, Lucy." She drew Thad close. "This is my son, Thad."

"Nice to meet you, Thad." Lucy grinned at the young boy, then glanced past them to Eben.

Deborah gestured toward him. "This is Eben Graber, my new neighbor."

Lucy extended her hand. "Nice to meet you, Eben."

"And you, Lucy," he said, shaking her hand.

"You must be tired and frozen from your long journey," Deborah told her. "Please come inside where it's warm. Or *will* be warm shortly, now that the fire is going."

"Thank you. I am grateful. I can no longer feel my fingers." Lucy held up her hands and laughed. "I wondered if I would ever arrive here." She retrieved her bag from the car and handed the driver some bills.

"Here, let me get that for you." Eben stepped forward and took the bag.

When his frame blocked Lucy from Deborah's view, Lucy mouthed, "What are you doing?" He shook his head. Now was not the time.

He and Lucy had agreed beforehand that she would keep her cell phone handy, but mute the volume so he could text her when they needed to communicate. Yet after what had happened tonight, he couldn't wait that long. He'd have to find a private moment with her before he left.

"Are you hungry?" Deborah asked once everyone was inside.

"I am. It has been hours since my last meal." Lucy glanced around. "You have a lovely home, Deborah."

"Denki," Deborah said with a smile.

Coming from an Amish background, Eben had worked with Lucy to prepare her, yet she had confessed to finding everything about the plain life confusing. To an outsider, the way of life seemed old-fashioned and strange, but Eben found himself increasingly drawn to it, remembering the days when he'd lived on his grandparents' farm. Life had been so simple back then.

With Lucy securely in place, he felt comfortable enough to leave. Plenty of surveillance photos and data waited for him at the house.

"Well, I should head out so Lucy can settle in," he told Deborah. "Thank you for the coffee and the company." He removed the car keys from his pocket, then added, "Make sure you lock the door so the wind doesn't blow it open again during the night."

"Did something happen earlier?" Lucy asked, in a tone that said she'd picked up on his message.

Deborah appeared embarrassed by the incident but explained.

"I am sure the wind is the culprit, but it never hurts to be careful," Lucy said. As a trained agent, she would do everything in her power to protect Deborah and Thad. He prayed it would be enough, because the news of Benson's early release had him worried.

Deborah retrieved her cloak and followed him out into the bitter cold, leaving Eben with the impression she wasn't ready to let him go, and, against his better judgment, his heart swelled with happiness.

"Thank you for bringing Thad and me home tonight," she said as she walked him to the car.

He hit the unlock button. "You're welcome. I've enjoyed meeting you and your son. He's a great boy."

She smiled up at him. "He is. He misses his Daed so much, though. I wish . . ." Her voice trailed off, and he wondered what she'd left unsaid. "Well, I should go back inside. Thad will talk Lucy's ear off if left on his own for long."

He smiled at her description and then touched her arm. "Be safe, Deborah. If you need anything at all, I'm just down the road."

She stared into his eyes a bit too long, then slowly nodded. "I know you are, and I am grateful for the offer. Denki, Eben."

He didn't move until she'd gone inside and closed the door. He hated leaving her. The instant connection he felt with Deborah couldn't be explained.

Somehow feeling the cold more sharply in her absence, Eben

drove the short distance to the Glick place. The house had sat empty for a number of years and showed signs of neglect.

When he'd first been told about the assignment and the home in which he would be staying, the joy he'd experienced at the thought of being back among the Amish surprised him.

The headlights of the car swept over the dark house. He retrieved his flashlight and went inside. He'd briefly seen the house earlier in the day. Though small, it would serve his purpose well. Lighting the lanterns the family had left behind, he surveyed the work needed to make the place livable while on assignment. Eben welcomed the task.

He'd start in the great room. Tomorrow he'd go into town and buy the boards to replace some bad floorboards in there. He carried in some of the supplies he'd brought with him for the stay and unrolled his sleeping bag in front of the woodstove.

The day had been an exhausting one, yet Eben's thoughts wouldn't let him rest. Deborah was foremost on his mind. Something about the beautiful Amish widow drew him in and made him want to get to know her better. More than that, he wanted to protect her, to keep her and her son safe.

Eben gave himself a mental shake. He was no longer Amish. And he had a job to do.

The fear on Thad's face earlier assured him the boy had witnessed something in the woods before he'd left his coat behind. Then the open door. His instincts screamed that Benson was the culprit. He and Lucy would have to be watchful because it was only a matter of time before Benson made his move—and when he did, Eben would be there to catch him.

3

"Thad, time for morning devotions." Deborah nudged her son's arm.

Thad put down the book on fishing that once belonged to his Daed and prepared to listen.

Deborah opened the Bible and sat down in front of the fire while Lucy slid into the second rocker.

Normally, she read the morning scripture in the language of the plain people, but out of respect to Lucy she would use English, a language she usually reserved for conversing with the Englisch tourists who visited her shop. Lucy had confessed to being unschooled in Pennsylvania German since she was from Canada.

At first, Deborah worried it might be difficult for them to communicate, but nothing was further from the truth. She and Lucy had managed nicely in English. It surprised her how easily they'd taken to each other right from the start, staying up late into the night, talking and laughing like a couple of teenagers.

Opening the Bible to Psalms, she found one of Peter's favorite scriptures, Psalms 5:3. *My voice You shall hear in the morning, O Lord; in the morning I will direct it to You, and I will look up.*

How many times had she heard Peter recite that verse, his eyes shining with sincerity? Peter had lived those words. She missed him so much that at times it was physically painful. She cleared her throat and said, "Time for prayer."

Thad and Lucy nodded and bowed their heads.

"*Gött*, help us each to seek You first in the morning and listen to

Your will for our lives all day long. Amen." She closed the Bible, then rose to her feet. "Time to get dressed for school, Thad. Off you go."

"Aw, Mamm. Why can't I stay home with Lucy today? It's her first day here."

She shook her head. "Not today. We need to let Lucy settle in."

Lucy smiled her gratitude. "Denki, Deborah. The trip here proved a stressful one." She ruffled Thad's hair. "And we'll have plenty of time to spend together. I'm sure you will be sick of me by the time I leave."

Thad grumbled all the way to his room and Deborah smothered a laugh. "He really is happy to have you here. So am I." She crossed to the front door. Removing her worn cloak from the wall peg, she slipped it around her shoulders, dreading the chilly morning. "I will be back as soon as I have finished the morning chores," she assured Lucy, then lifted the lantern from its hanging spot and lit it.

"I can help if you'd like." Lucy followed her to the door. "I want to earn my keep."

Deborah smiled. "That is very kind, but not necessary. You stay inside where it's warm. I'll be back soon." Clutching her cloak tight, she hurried outside. A bitter wind howled with renewed force. Yet despite the winter chill, this was one of Deborah's favorite times of the day, with the world just rising from its slumber. A new day made her feel as if anything was possible.

She headed for the barn. Even through the thick boots she wore, the cold nipped at her toes. Several inches of snow clung to everything within the lantern's glow. Winter came on quickly here in the valley and plenty of things needed to be done around the place to prepare for it.

Days of freezing weather made it hard to heat the house. Thankfully, the men of the community graciously provided her with enough firewood to last throughout the winter. Her summer garden had yielded plenty of vegetables for canning. She and Thad would be fine, but the animals needed food for the long months ahead. She would need to buy hay and oats from the Strubhars, and money was tight. A kind widower, Thomas Strubhar, and his sons had helped Deborah a lot after Peter's death. If she bartered some of her canned goods for feed, perhaps it would be enough to survive the winter months.

Deborah drew in a breath and slowly released it. Gött would provide as He always did. She just had to keep her faith stronger than her fears. If necessary, she'd take on more work. They would be fine.

In the distance, the Sangre de Cristo Mountains jutted up against the dark sky. Here was where she felt the closest to Gött. Today, they had received a reprieve from the snowfall. The sky above was filled with stars. She loved living in the vast, open spaces of Colorado and couldn't imagine life anywhere other than her San Luis Valley community.

The late-night conversation with Lucy began to catch up with her, and she stifled a yawn. Over Kaffe and the cake Deborah had prepared especially for their visitor, Lucy had asked dozens of questions about the community, Deborah's life here, and even about her late husband, Peter, a difficult subject to discuss even after more than a year.

Tears stung her eyes, and she swiped them away. No matter how much one dwelt on the past, it could not be rewritten. As her Grossmammi had been fond of saying, those who lived in the past missed Gött's blessing for the day.

She reached for the barn door when something out of place captured her attention. Footprints. All around. The incident with Thad and the open door the night before crept into her thoughts unwelcome. She glanced around, suddenly nervous.

Squinting into the nearby woods, her heart leapt to her throat as a man ran from the edge of the barn, zigzagging through the woods. No one from the community would leave without first speaking. That man was up to no good.

As he drove down the pitted dirt road connecting his place to Deborah's, something in the woods grabbed Eben's attention. Though it was almost dawn, the sun had not quite risen on the horizon. Darkness still clung to the surrounding countryside. Eben peered through the passenger window. A light disappeared into the woods separating their homes. He braked the car hard, parked, and gave chase on foot, a difficult task with the thick snow accumulation in the woods.

When he crested the hill the light was gone. He aimed his flashlight all around—it was still dark under the trees—but the person appeared to have vanished.

A hunter? The unease in the pit of his stomach wouldn't allow him to accept that. Eben hurried back to the car and texted Lucy. When she didn't answer, he drove as fast as possible to Deborah's.

As he drew near the house, Eben spotted Deborah running from the barn. He screeched to a halt and killed the engine, then rushed to her side.

"What happened?" he asked, clasping her arms. His head raced with possibilities.

Drawing in a shaky breath, she shook her head and it was as if a mask of calm fell over her face. "Nothing." She stepped back, putting distance between them. It wasn't the truth. "I did not expect to see you today."

He released her arms, but his mind wouldn't let go of the man in the woods. "I needed some supplies for the house so I thought I'd stop by and see how things went with your visitor." Something had happened. What wasn't she telling him?

Deborah glanced over her shoulder, then started walking again.

Eben fell in next to her, slowing his footsteps to match hers.

"*Gut.* Lucy is a wonderful houseguest. Would you like to join us for breakfast? I made an egg casserole and there is plenty," she said without looking at him.

"I'd like that very much," he told her, the invitation surprising him. "I had planned to grab something at the diner, but your breakfast casserole sounds too good to pass up."

She stopped and stared at him, a hint of a smile lifting the corners of her mouth. His heart skipped a beat at its appearance.

"*Gut.* Thad will be pleased to see you again."

It was on the tip of his tongue to ask if she was pleased as well, but she opened the door and went inside. With another nervous look around, he followed, waiting as she extinguished the lantern and hung it up.

Thad was perched on one of the rockers close to the fire talking to Lucy. Both glanced up as he and Deborah came in.

"I hope you haven't been talking Lucy's ears off." Deborah leaned down and kissed her son's cheek. "Help me set the table. Eben is joining us this morning."

The boy's face lit up. "Can we take another ride in your car?" Thad's enthusiasm was contagious.

"Now, Thad, we don't want to impose," Deborah chided. "Besides, you have school today."

Eben chuckled, shaking his head. "It's okay. I'm glad you enjoyed the car ride. If it's okay with your mother, I'd be happy to give you both a ride into town. I'm going that way myself."

"Can we, Mamm?" Thad begged.

"We will see. Right now, I need you to set the table."

Thad raced to do as she asked, no doubt thinking it might help his cause.

When mother and son were out of earshot, Eben slipped into the boy's vacated chair.

"I'm sorry I wasn't able to text you back," Lucy whispered. "I couldn't get away. Did you get a good look at the man?"

Eben made sure they couldn't be overheard. "No, he was too far away. Did you hear anything unusual outside?"

She shook her head. "As far as I know, it's been quiet. Once the Albrechts are gone, I'll take a look around outside to be certain."

He nodded. "Good idea." Although it wasn't the answer he'd hoped for, it would have to do.

"Breakfast is ready. Come to the table," Deborah called from the kitchen as she carefully removed the breakfast casserole and placed it on top of the stove.

The smell took him back once more. As a child, he had loved each moment he spent with his grandparents. His Grossmammi would prepare her special breakfast casserole especially for him, knowing how he loved it.

"Eben?" The past evaporated before his eyes when he realized Deborah was trying to get his attention.

"I'm sorry," he said with a twist of his lips. "I'm a million miles away."

As he sank into a chair at the table, his thoughts fast-forwarded to the long days ahead of him once his time here ended. He'd face another case. Another victim. For a while, he'd told himself that his choices made him happy, that the work he did was important. But the longing to return to his Amish roots waited for him wherever he went.

Deborah dished out the casserole, and with Thad's help, carried the plates to the table while Lucy poured milk for Thad and coffee for the adults.

"This looks amazing," Eben told Deborah. Though he hadn't mentioned his plain past before, he wondered if she guessed.

Once the women were seated, Deborah nodded to Thad. "Let's pray."

The boy bowed his head and lowered his hands in preparation for the silent prayer.

No matter how many times Eben swallowed, the lump in his throat wouldn't go away. He bowed his head, a weary breath escaping. For a long time after his father's excommunication, Eben had given up on Gött. Growing up, he'd believed in the goodness of Gött, but how could a loving Father allow their family to be torn apart in such a tragic way?

His parents, on the other hand, had never abandoned Gött. Their faith made him ashamed of his doubts. His Daed had moved the family to a rural community some distance from the Charlotte County Amish district. Caleb went to work for a farmer while his Mamm cleaned houses. Yet they'd continued to abide by the rules of the Ordnung, living simple lives and putting their faith in Gött.

The prayer ended with Eben fighting back overwhelming emotions that threatened to become tears. He glanced up and found Deborah watching him, compassion etched on her face. Had she seen the pain he couldn't hide?

"Please eat," she said softly, then waited until he'd taken a bite before doing so herself.

"When did you learn how to drive?" Thad asked with a mouthful of the casserole muffling his words.

"Swallow before speaking, Thad."

Thad quickly complied. "Were you my age?" he asked hopefully. "I can drive the buggy all by myself—when Mamm lets me."

"Sorry to disappoint, but I was seventeen," he said and watched Thad's smile fade.

Thoughts of the first year after they'd left the plain life came to mind. Eben hadn't known what to do with himself, torn between his past and the unknown future. His Daed had taught him how to drive. With his license, he'd found a job and put himself through college. Then, when the FBI came to his campus to recruit, Eben became drawn to the work they did.

"I was about eighteen when I got my license, though most kids get theirs around sixteen. I guess I'm a slow learner." When the past and all its regrets pressed in, Eben scraped back his chair and carried his plate to the sink to wash it.

"You do not have to do that. You are our guest," Deborah said, following him to the sink.

"And I can wash a plate." He took the one she held in her hand. "It's the least I can do to thank you for allowing me to share this wonderful meal with you."

Deborah hesitated a second, clearly trying to decide whether to argue with him, then grabbed a dish towel. "It is good to have a full table again," she said as she dried the dish he'd washed. She appeared to be distracted by something.

For a while, they worked together in companionable silence. He'd forgotten how fulfilling it was to do a simple task like washing dishes.

"Would you mind helping me in the barn for a moment?" she asked once they'd finished the cleanup.

The strange request seemed to confirm something had happened earlier outside the barn.

"Not at all. I'm happy to help."

Deborah covered her relief badly. "Thank you." Without another word, she dried her hands, then headed to the door, where they both put on their outerwear.

Thad grabbed his coat and started to put it on, but Deborah stopped him. "I need you to wait inside with Lucy this time. I will feed the chickens and gather the eggs today."

Surprise shown on the boy's face, but he did as his mother asked.

Deborah stepped out into the cold with Eben at her side. As they left the porch, she said, "I just need to gather the eggs. It shouldn't take long."

Sunlight glistened off the snow. As they drew close to the barn, Eben spotted something alarming—two sets of footprints in the snow. One was likely Deborah's, but who had made the other?

Fear settled in deep. He'd had good reason to be concerned about the light in the woods. Someone had been wandering around outside the house. His gut told him it was Benson.

Eben unhooked the board holding the door shut. It protested as he pulled it open. Inside, shadows clung to everything.

Deborah went over to the chicken coop and gathered eggs, placing them in her apron.

The Amish life was not an easy one. Just keeping a farm going meant long hours and hard work. He couldn't imagine how Deborah managed alone.

Eben glanced around at the familiar Amish setting that tugged at his heart.

"Is something wrong?" Deborah asked, her voice calling him back to the present.

He shook his head. "No, I'm just remembering the last time I milked a cow. It's been years." A wry smile touched his face when he realized he'd slipped up with the admission. He opened the door and they went outside.

"Where did you learn how to milk a cow?" she asked as they started for the house, her gaze locked on his. "It's not something most Englisch know how to do."

His conscience warred with his job. However, if he ever wanted to earn her trust, she deserved to hear the truth. At least as much of it as he could tell her. "I used to be Amish," he admitted, then watched as surprise flashed across her face.

"Why did you leave?" she asked softly.

Speaking the truth was hard, but he had to try. "My family left the faith when I was seventeen, before I was baptized."

She drew in a breath. "But you did not want to leave."

He looked away. Swallowed. "No. It was the hardest thing I've ever done. My world collapsed when I found out we were leaving. My grandparents didn't want to go with us, so we were forced to leave them behind. I never forgave myself for deserting them."

"Oh Eben," she murmured, taking a step closer. With sympathy shining on her pretty face, she placed a gentle hand on his arm. "I am sorry."

He bowed his head. "My Grossdaddi taught me so much. He was larger than life. When he passed away, I . . ." He couldn't finish, the pain still too fresh after all these years.

"I am sure he understood why you had to leave," she said quietly.

But she didn't know everything.

Shaking off the past, he forced a smile. "Sorry, I didn't mean to unload on you." He started walking again. She fell into step beside him, keeping her full attention on supporting the eggs in her apron. She was a lovely woman with a strength that ran deep.

Unexpectedly, she glanced his way and found him watching her. Eben forced his gaze away as he hurried ahead to open the door.

Balancing the eggs carefully, she moved past him into the house. Deborah's fresh clean scent reminded him of the outdoors, spices, and home.

With his heart pounding out a crazy beat, he drew in a breath and followed her to the kitchen, where she put the eggs away.

"Thad, it's time to leave for school," she called out to the boy, who was reading by the fire.

He closed his book and came into the kitchen. "I'm ready. Can we ride with Eben?"

With the unexplained man in the woods, Eben didn't think it wise for them to walk.

"Deborah, why don't you let me drive you and Thad? I'm going that way anyway and it would be no trouble."

She hesitated. He sensed she wanted to accept. "I wouldn't want to keep you from your duties."

"I promise you aren't keeping me from anything important."

"Okay, but just this once," Deborah told him, a look of relief on her face.

He'd do his best to convince her otherwise, or at least try to persuade her to take the buggy in the future. Walking left them exposed. There were too many places for Benson to hide.

Deborah helped Thad into his new coat. "We will need to pay Henry Yoder a visit soon to thank him properly for returning your father's coat to you. Perhaps I can take him some of my chokecherry jam," she told the boy.

Eben immediately went on alert. "Who's Henry?" he asked to cover his concern.

"A new member of our community. Last week, Henry returned my husband's coat to Thad." Deborah smiled down at the boy. "He found it at the site where Peter had been working." She stopped and swallowed hard, then continued. "Henry said he'd forgotten about the coat until recently. As a carpenter, he and my husband worked on some of the same jobs."

Eben had visited Henry's home the day before and no one appeared to be home. With Benson roaming the area, he couldn't allow Deborah and the boy to make that visit. It was too risky. He'd have to find some way to change her mind.

Gathering her things, Deborah faced Lucy. "I truly hate leaving you alone for the whole day. Are you sure you won't come with us?"

Lucy gave her a smile. "Don't worry about me. I will be fine on my own. I plan to write some letters home and maybe read a book. Perhaps I'll take a short nap later. I could take care of the housework if you tell me what needs to be done," she added, but Deborah shook her head.

"That's not necessary. It's your first day here, and I'm sure you must still be tired from your long trip. But you should lock the door after we leave. I would hate for it to blow open and wake you from your sleep."

With another smile, Lucy said, "I promise I will lock the door. I'll be fine."

"All right, if you're sure. We'll see you later," Deborah said.

Together, she, Eben, and Thad headed out into the chilly gray morning.

Once Thad was secured in the back seat, Eben reached for the door handle at the same time as Deborah, his hand briefly covering hers. He could feel the rough skin of someone who had worked hard most of her life and his chest constricted. For a moment, he lost himself in huge eyes against pale skin.

Unable to stop himself, he scraped back an escaping strand of her hair and she froze at his touch. Immediately he stepped back, regretting his impulsiveness. Deborah quickly opened the door and climbed inside while Eben steeled himself to face her again.

What was wrong with him? He was there to protect her and bring Victor Benson to justice. Nothing more. Once he accomplished that, he'd return to Washington, D.C., and his life there.

Eben opened the door and got behind the wheel, keeping his attention on the path ahead and not on the woman at his side.

"Why does a car have two pedals?" Thad asked, his innocent question breaking the awkward silence.

Eben was happy for the distraction. "Because one makes the car go and the other makes it stop."

Beside him, Deborah shifted in her seat. He sensed she wanted to ask him something.

"Just say it," he said.

"Okay. Why did you choose to move to our community?" Her forehead crinkled in a frown, her doubts clear. "You haven't lived the plain life in a long time. Why come back to it now?"

Eben scrambled to come up with a believable answer. "I guess I needed a break from my life. Things got a little hectic, and I'd visited the area once before and liked it. So, I bought the Glick farm." He shrugged, hating the lie.

"Where did you live before?" Her gaze held his, doubt evident in her expression.

"My family lived in Virginia. My father and mother are still there."

"Did they regret leaving the faith?" she asked, believing his story.

He nodded. "They did. Even though it wasn't possible to return, my Daed still abides by the rules of the Ordnung."

Her eyes widened. "He is Amish at heart."

"He is." Eben thought about his father. Though he'd gone against the bishop's ruling and let pride stop him from apologizing for his sin, Caleb had always longed to return to his old life. His Mamm as well. Many times, Eben's mother wept late at night, missing her family.

He cast a glance Deborah's way. She was so easy to talk to. Eben found himself rattling on about growing up in his community. "My grandfather owned a dairy farm and there was always plenty of work to do, but it was *gut* work. Satisfying work. For a while, we lived close to my grandparents until my father decided to leave the faith."

"That must have been hard," she said. "I cannot imagine living any other way."

His hands tightened on the wheel. At one time, he couldn't imagine a life outside of the Amish world either. Even now, he longed for it.

"Yes. It's more than just a way of life, though. It's part of who you are inside."

Was it his imagination or were there tears in her eyes? "After Peter died, I didn't know how I would make it without him. I felt so lost. But everyone in the community stepped in to help." She lowered her chin to her chest. "It made the loss easier."

He remembered the time after his grandfather's passing. While his family no longer belonged to the community, the people of the church district had gone out of their way to help them. Knowing there were so many others who would pitch in whenever life got hard was one of the things he missed most about being Amish.

The tiny one-room schoolhouse appeared in front of them. Eben stopped the car in front. Several children stood outside waiting for class to begin.

"Looks like you're right on time." Eben glanced in the rearview mirror as Thad unbuckled his seatbelt and bolted from the car.

"Thad, wait!" Deborah tried to stop him, but Thad paid no attention. He bounded toward another boy, gesturing at the car.

She shook her head. "That's David Zook, Thad's best friend. Be prepared. David will want a ride in your car soon."

Eben chuckled and put the car in motion. "I remember how I felt the first time I rode in a car. It will fade soon enough." He chanced a look her way. "You know, it's no trouble for me to drive you both each day, at least while it's so cold. I'll be starting work at the diner soon. And it would be nice to have the company on the drive. I've spent a lot of time alone. It's nice to have someone to talk to."

She smiled sweetly. "That is kind of you, but I don't think Bishop Timothy would approve of us riding in a car every day."

He hadn't taken the bishop's position into account. "Well, at least let me give you a ride home today. I plan to speak with Samuel about the work at the diner after I finish at the store. Maybe I can start on some of the expansion today. I can work on my house in the evenings."

She didn't answer, but kept her focus on the road ahead. He had no idea what she was thinking.

Eben stopped the car in front of her shop and glanced up at it. For reasons he couldn't explain, the feeling they were being watched wouldn't leave his head.

Deborah must have sensed his unease because she shifted in her seat. "Is something wrong?"

He couldn't look at her and keep the truth from showing. "No. I was just thinking how lucky you and Thad are to live in such a beautiful community." Without waiting for her response, he got out of the car and went around to her door. While he told himself he was only concerned for her safety, in truth, he wasn't ready to say goodbye just yet.

He could not deny his attraction to her. He'd never had this reaction to a woman before and it scared him. He'd need to tread carefully. Whatever he thought he felt, he couldn't afford to become emotionally involved. It might end up costing Deborah her life.

4

Removing the key from her pocket, Deborah started up the steps to the shop. Once she unlocked the door, she stepped inside, then faced Eben once more, unsure what to say to him.

When he came in and closed the door, the space between them became too small and she stepped back.

Though tiny, the shop was neat and Deborah was proud to call it hers. Several quilts made by the local women were on display in the window along with a few of the dresses she'd made herself. The shop contained rows of material and threads, along with other sewing tools.

Opening Albrecht's Fabrics had been a dream of Deborah's since she had been a little girl. The joy of making her own clothes was something her Mamm had instilled in her at a young age. She still remembered her Mamm patiently helping her with her stitches.

The chill inside the shop seeped through her clothes, and Deborah went over to the woodstove in the center of the room.

"Here, let me help you." Eben took the logs from her and stacked them in the stove, his jacket stretching over muscular arms as he worked. The scent of his soap reminded her of what it was like to have a strong, *gut* man around. She touched a hand to her flamed cheeks and forced herself to stop staring.

"That should keep the place warm for a bit." Satisfied, he straightened.

"Denki," she murmured.

"You are welcome." He headed for the door, then swung to face her again. "I'll pick you and Thad up later this afternoon." She started to protest but he held up a hand. "It's no trouble, Deborah, and I'd enjoy the company."

He opened the door. She wasn't ready to let him go. "Eben, wait."

He spun around, and a silly part of her wondered if he was as loath to leave her as she was for him to go.

She shook her head and tried to find the right words. "No, that is—there is a dinner tonight," she blurted out and saw surprise in his eyes. "It's at the school if you would like to come." She bit her bottom lip. Why had she invited him? As an outsider, he would no doubt feel ill at ease among the Amish, even though he'd once been part of their world.

His gaze held hers. She could see the struggle going on inside him.

"You don't have to come," she quickly assured him. "I'm not sure why I mentioned it, truly. You must have other things to do."

Eben softly closed the door and came over to her, touching her hand ever so gently. "I don't, and I would love to come," he said with a smile that lit up his handsome face.

She couldn't help it. Her heart beat wildly as joy thundered through her. "*Gut*," she said, ashamed that her voice trembled.

Silence stretched between them, and try as she might, she couldn't think of a way to break it.

Finally, he did. "Well, I should be going." The roughness in his voice matched hers. "I want to see what Samuel has planned for the expansion. It will be good to work with my hands again." Yet he still didn't move.

She nodded, clutching a piece of fabric to her chest to steady her nervous hands. "He is happy to have your help. Samuel and Gertie have been talking about the expansion for a long time. It has been a dream for them since they took over the business from Gertie's parents. They purchased the empty store next to the diner last year. The plan is to break down the wall separating the two spaces and connect them."

"That will make a nice restaurant. I look forward to helping Samuel and Gertie with their dream. I will see you later this afternoon. What time do you close the shop?"

She told him, then, with a final wave, he headed out into the cold morning.

Still holding the cloth, Deborah went to the window and watched as Eben disappeared into the diner. The aprons for the upcoming wedding needed finishing, yet all she could think about was this man who had suddenly come into her life.

Barely a year passed since she'd lost Peter. It was much too soon for her to have feelings for another man, yet she couldn't deny she enjoyed spending time with Eben. He made her feel safe.

She shook her head at her foolishness. Eben carried a lot of baggage, struggling to find his place in the world—much like she did. He hadn't told her everything about his past—though they'd barely met, so why should he? She had Thad to think about, though. She couldn't afford to take chances with her son by letting someone with issues into their lives.

With a deep sigh, Deborah tossed the fabric onto the counter. She had work to finish. There was no time for daydreaming. Picking up the apron she'd worked on the previous day, she took it back to the shop and sat in her favorite chair facing the breathtaking Sangre de Cristo Mountains. The mountains were as much a part of her world as the Amish way of life she cherished.

With great care, Deborah finished the apron, then held it up to inspect. She hoped Faith would be pleased with her efforts. The white organdy apron would look lovely against the sky-blue wedding dress Deborah had completed for Faith earlier in the week. After the wedding, the dress would make a fine Sunday garment.

She gently folded the apron and placed it in the box holding the wedding dress. Retrieving the bolt of white organdy from the storage room, she brought out the pattern she would use for the capes for the bride and her attendants to wear over their dresses. Instead of a veil, Faith would wear a black prayer covering to differentiate from the white Kapps of her *Newehockers*.

As she worked, she thought about the time before her own wedding. She'd been so proud when the news of her and Peter's upcoming marriage was published at the end of the church service. With her Mamm's help, Deborah had lovingly sewn her and her attendants' dresses. Then, the day of her wedding arrived in late November. She had been so nervous and so in love with Peter.

Tears filled her eyes. They'd both been so excited for their future together. Now, she had to find a way to be content with her life without Peter and not go searching for things lost. Gött would direct her path.

As Deborah cut out the first cape, a noise coming from somewhere behind the shop drew her attention. It sounded like something was rummaging in the trash behind the building. A hungry bear trying to find food?

Slowly, she eased to the back door. She saw nothing through the window. With shaking fingers, she slid the lock free, drew in a shaky breath, and inched the door open. Nothing appeared out of place. The breath she held inside slowly slipped away, frosting the air in front of her.

As she turned to go back inside, something caught her attention. A familiar sense of dread settled in her stomach as she stared at fresh footprints in the snow heading around the side of the shop. At the side of the building, the steps veered to the left—straight for the school.

Thad!

Without thinking about her own safety, she sprinted toward the schoolhouse heedless of the cold. When she reached the school, the footprints turned toward the woods. First outside the barn and now this. Too many coincidences added up to trouble.

She hurried up the steps to the school and went inside. The teacher stopped in the middle of her lesson, surprised by Deborah's sudden appearance.

"Just a moment, children. Please start reading the next section in your books," Jemimah Swartzentruber said, recovering quickly. She hurried over to Deborah. "Was iss letz?"

Deborah pulled the younger woman out of earshot of her curious students. "Can you keep Thad inside today?"

"Of course. Is something wrong?" the young teacher asked.

Deborah wasn't sure how to answer. She had no proof the person who'd made the footprints meant them harm. "I am not sure. Perhaps I'm just being cautious, but still, I will come pick him up after school. I don't want him walking to the shop alone."

Jemimah willingly agreed and didn't pry, much to Deborah's relief. "The weather is supposed to turn ugly again today. I will keep all the Kinner inside to be safe," she said, her choice of words unsettling.

"Denki, Jemimah." She squeezed the younger woman's arm, then went back outside, drawing in crisp, clean air to clear her head. Was she overreacting?

As much as she wanted to believe so, she couldn't. The present chill in the air went much deeper than the cold. Something—or more likely some*one*—bad lingered nearby.

Eben had spent most of the day working alongside Samuel on the expansion of the diner until it was time to pick up Deborah and Thad. As they went over the plans for the new dining room, it was easy to get caught up in the excitement of what the diner would look like in the future and forget his true purpose here in the valley.

When he went to the fabric shop to drive Deborah and Thad home, Deborah appeared preoccupied by something.

Though Thad enjoyed the ride, asking dozens of questions, Deborah barely said a handful of words throughout the trip. He wanted to ask her what was troubling her, but their friendship was still too new.

Once they'd reached her home, Eben discreetly pulled Lucy aside to see if she'd learned anything useful in her search. She'd told him she'd followed the footprints through the woods, but lost them around the same place where Eben saw the light disappear. Was it Benson? Who else could it be?

As soon as he reached his house, he pulled out the case files and began pouring over them, all the while watching the clock. If he was smart, he'd stay home tonight and keep working the case. Not blur the lines between his job and his growing affection for Deborah any further. Yet as the appointed time for the dinner grew closer, Eben found he couldn't concentrate, and, with a frustrated grunt, he abandoned the files entirely. Grabbing his keys, he went outside and climbed inside the car while trying to ignore the warnings going around in his head.

Pulling the car up in front of the school, Eben counted at least ten buggies lined up outside. Doubts continued to plague him as he parked. Coming here tonight was a mistake. They would look at him and see him as an outsider. The distance between his life now and his Amish roots was an impossible chasm to cross.

He'd berated himself constantly since he'd accepted Deborah's invitation. He had sworn to protect her, and yet no matter how much he tried to convince himself otherwise, Eben couldn't deny the subtle longing he felt every time he gazed at her pretty face.

All the more reason to keep his distance. He should go back to the house. Make up some excuse why he couldn't attend. Lucy would be there to protect her. He should be working the case. Reviewing surveillance photos.

Guarding his heart.

He nearly reached for the gearshift, then pictured how vulnerable she'd looked when she asked him to attend. No matter what it cost him personally, he wouldn't disappoint her.

Eben yanked open the door and climbed out. Taking the steps slowly, he pushed the door open wide enough to enter. The tiny one-room schoolhouse was crowded with people. Like the many after-church meals he'd attended, the women gathered on one side of the building while the men chatted on the other.

Wooden benches lined both sides of the room. At one end, a long table loaded with food reminded him of all the dinners he'd attended in his youth. He'd loved those social gatherings. The feeling of being with people you loved and trusted ran deep.

People turned at his arrival and gaped. An Englischer at an Amish gathering was a rare thing.

Eben searched the room for a friendly face. Samuel stood in the corner surrounded by a group of men.

Scanning the room, he spotted Deborah talking with an elderly woman. She smiled sweetly at the woman. He'd thought about her smile a lot during the day. The way her golden-brown hair peeked out from underneath her bonnet. How her eyes brightened whenever she saw him.

When she looked up and found him watching her, that sparkle in her eyes made him believe his presence pleased her. A smiled creased his face. Coming inside had been the right decision after all.

The woman beside her said something and Deborah's gaze shot back to her as a delightful pink colored her cheeks.

A hand clamped down on his shoulder, and Eben whirled to find his new employer, Samuel, standing close with a grin on his face.

"Eben. I'm happy to see you here tonight. Come with me. I want to introduce you to some of the men in the community." Samuel led Eben to the group of men Samuel had been chatting with earlier. Would they ask him to leave? Treat him like an outsider?

Samuel interrupted the men's discussion by pulling Eben into the center of the group. The conversation abruptly ended. A hush fell over the gathering as they stared at Eben.

"This is Eben Graber. He will be helping me with the expansion on the diner. He's new to the community and has bought the Glicks' old place." Samuel introduced Eben to each of the men. One name in particular caught his attention—Matthew Albrecht.

Eben accepted the hand the elderly man offered. His beard held more gray than not, much like his hair.

"You are my daughter-in-law's new neighbor," Matthew said, and Eben's brows slanted together. "Deborah Albrecht. She and her son, Thad, live close to the Glicks' old homestead." Matthew nodded to where Deborah still chatted with the woman. "That's her speaking with my wife."

His attention reverted back to Deborah. He couldn't take his eyes off her.

"The Glicks were *gut* people. It saddened everyone in the community when the couple passed away just a few short months apart. The house has been empty far too long," Matthew continued.

"There's still a lot to be done to make it livable again, but I don't mind. I enjoy the work."

"Ja, it is *gut* work," Samuel patted Eben's shoulder. "And I am grateful to have your help at the diner. Expanding has been a dream of ours since Gertie's parents gave us the diner."

"Well, I look forward to it," Eben said and meant it. While the repairs at the house were many, they wouldn't take too long to complete. Today, he'd managed to repair the floor in the great room and finish the cabinets. Several windows were broken around the place. He'd work on fixing them soon. Though the work was only part of his cover and had to be done around his working the case, it was satisfying nonetheless.

As he listened to the men talk in English for his benefit, he realized he enjoyed their conversation. The camaraderie, the sense of community that the Amish shared was something he hadn't found anywhere else.

"Ach, Bishop Timothy. How are you tonight?" Samuel asked as another man joined their group.

"I am *gut*." The bishop nodded, his keen eyes honing in on Eben with curiosity.

"This is Eben Graber, the carpenter I was telling you about, Bishop," Samuel explained

Eben dreaded the bishop's reaction. In the church district where he'd grown up, the bishop had ruled the church with a firm hand.

Bishop Timothy stuck out his hand, a smile on his face. "It is nice to meet you, Eben. Samuel tells me *gut* things about you. You are welcome here."

"Thank you," Eben replied, clasping the bishop's hand. "It's good to meet you as well."

"I hope you are finding everything you need. Samuel says you wish to make the Glick place a working farm again?" The interest in the bishop's eyes was genuine. In some ways, the man reminded him of his grandfather. He was tall and sturdily built, with a headful of white hair and a long, pale beard to match.

"That is my plan and I am grateful to Samuel for the job. It will help pay for the repairs."

The bishop nodded. "Samuel is a *gut* man, and we are happy to have him in our community." With a final jovial nod, Bishop Timothy moved on to the next group of men.

As Samuel focused on what the man next to him was saying, Eben turned away, drawing in a steadying breath. He'd had no idea how difficult this assignment would be when he agreed to go undercover. It was forcing him to deal with emotions he'd stuffed down deep through the years.

Eben noticed Deborah standing alone and excused himself, making his way over to her. As he drew close, she glanced up. The uncertainty he saw in her made him wish he could read her thoughts.

He stopped next to her looking around for Lucy. With everything going on, he'd expected his partner to be glued to Deborah's side.

"Good evening," he said while watching the emotions pass across her face. Doubt, worry—and something more.

"Good evening, Eben." Her voice sounded slightly breathless. "I'm happy you decided to come."

"It's a nice turnout. Where's Thad?"

Deborah pointed to a group of boys over by the blackboard. Thad, along with the boy he'd seen the day before, David, were playing jacks.

"He looks like he's having fun. Where's your guest?"

"Lucy had a headache and decided to stay home for the evening."

Eben hid his surprise with difficulty. Why would Lucy choose to stay behind? Unless she wanted to take a closer look around. Perhaps she'd found out something.

Deborah fidgeted with her hands, which appeared to be what she did when something troubled her.

"What's wrong?" he asked and prayed she would trust him with the truth. "If something is troubling you, perhaps I can assist."

She drew in a breath and shook her head. "To be honest, I'm not sure what to make of it. This morning, before you came to the house—" Tension tightened the fine lines around her eyes and mouth. "Eben, there were footprints all around outside the barn again." She lifted her shoulders. "I should have told you earlier, but I thought I was overreacting, and . . ."

"And you didn't fully trust me," he supplied for her, clasping her hand in his, a smile on his face that she'd told him at all. "It's okay, I get it. I hope you will trust me now. I only want to help."

She gently pulled her hand free. "I can think of no reason anyone would be outside my barn during the night. And then after you left the shop this morning, I heard something out back. When I went out, I saw more footprints heading from the back of the shop to the school." She paused to gauge his reaction. "But perhaps I am overreacting. The two may not be connected."

As much as he wanted to reassure her, he couldn't. Eben was convinced the man he'd seen roaming around the woods before dawn was up to no good. Now, someone was lurking around Deborah's shop and the school. He was certain it was Benson.

With Deborah waiting for his answer, he decided to downplay the events. "I'm sure it was nothing to worry about. Perhaps a curious visitor."

Letting go of his concerns was difficult, but he didn't want Deborah picking up on them. He'd keep careful watch over her and Thad the rest of the evening. Perhaps he could convince her to let him give them a ride home.

Thad tugged at his sleeve, drawing his attention away from Deborah. "Can David see your car? He's never been in one before."

David stood next to Thad, twisting his black felt hat in his hands, his eyes hopeful.

"Sure." Eben grinned at the two youngsters. "Come on, boys."

"Yippee!" Thad whooped and the two practically ran over each other to be the first out the door.

Eben chuckled at their excitement, then smiled at Deborah. "I'll be right back."

She nodded, her eyes sparkling. He loved the way her smile lit up her face and erased the worry he'd seen earlier. As he continued to stare, she touched her hands to her cheeks and turned away, embarrassed. Pivoting on his heel, he followed the boys outside without another word while chaos controlled his emotions.

The two waited by the car, barely able to contain their enthusiasm. Eben hid his amusement as he unlocked the door and opened it.

"Hop in, David. Take a look around."

Thad didn't have to be invited. He clambered inside and grabbed the steering wheel. "Zoom, zoom!" He twisted the wheel and pretended to drive.

David, a little more hesitant, slowly hopped up beside Thad, peering around in awe as Thad explained what each of the instruments did.

After bombarding Eben with a dozen questions, the boys abandoned their adventure when Deborah came out to collect them for the meal.

"I hope they weren't too much of a handful," she asked as they followed the boys inside.

"Not at all. It's nice to see their curiosity and excitement."

Eben held the door open for her and she slipped past him, ducking her head so he couldn't see her expression.

Much like the after-church meals, the men were served first and seated at one table, and then the women and children ate. Eben found a seat next to Samuel and bowed his head for the silent prayer.

While he enjoyed the conversation and the men treated him respectfully instead of as an unwelcome outsider, what Deborah had told him earlier stuck in his head. Someone had been outside her shop, then near the school, and he had a good guess who it might have been.

The fellowship after the meal lingered for several hours. When Eben noticed Deborah preparing to leave, he went over to her. He couldn't allow her to make the trip home alone. Not after what she'd told him.

"Why don't you let me follow you and Thad home tonight? You can drive your buggy and I'll follow."

A tiny frown line appeared between her brows. "It wouldn't be proper," she said, but he could see the uncertainty in her eyes. Clearly what had happened earlier had bothered her, as well it should.

"I'll give you a head start of five minutes, then I'll leave too. Please. I'd feel better knowing you got home safely."

She looked into his eyes, then gave a nod. He started toward Samuel and the bishop, who were still chatting at a table, lingering over cups of coffee. He heard Thad call out a goodbye and he turned to wave, as Deborah, pulling her cloak around her shoulders, left.

That was the longest five minutes of his life. Mercifully, the bishop stood. "It's time I headed home," he said. "Samuel, Eben, I'll see you around the diner. I could use some of Gertie's chicken and noodles and a piece of pie once your renovations are complete."

"You can think about food after tonight?" Samuel said, rubbing his belly.

"I can always think of food," the bishop said.

Eben said his goodbyes and strode out to his car as fast as he could without drawing attention to himself. It was an easy matter to catch up to her buggy on the road, so few people lived out this way.

When they arrived, he asked Deborah and Thad to wait in the buggy while he checked out the house. He cleared it, then returned to the buggy and gave her a nod. She blew out a breath of relief.

He offered his hand to help her step down, and she clasped it. He could feel callouses on her fingers, proof of how hard her life had been since her husband's death. She deserved so much more.

What had started as another assignment was quickly becoming something else. For as long as he could remember, the job had consumed him, making his personal life nonexistent. Now, being with Deborah and Thad made him wish for things that didn't seem possible. When this assignment ended, how could he return to his old life—and not regret leaving theirs?

5

Someone knocked on the door. Deborah hurried to the window to check but Thad was too fast.

"Eben!" He raced past her and started to open it, but Deborah caught his arm.

"Wait," she told him. Since the footprints outside the barn and the ones near the shop, Deborah hadn't been able to relax. She glanced out the window to make sure it was Eben.

Her son's bond with the man had continued to grow with each moment they spent together and it troubled her. The boy still cried at nights when he thought she didn't hear. She wouldn't have his heart broken again when Eben grew tired of the plain life and returned to his Englisch one.

Smoothing her dress in place, Deborah braced to face him again and pulled the door open.

"*Gut* morning," he said with a smile.

"*Gut* morning to you." Her breath hitched in her throat and she prayed he didn't notice her nerves.

Thad grabbed Eben's hand and dragged him behind him. "Hurry, Eben. Mamm has breakfast ready."

Deborah drew in a breath and closed the door. "Thad, perhaps Eben has other things to do today." She waited for Eben's answer with hope in her heart.

"There is always time for breakfast, especially if it's scrapple as my nose seems to think."

She couldn't help but smile. "It is. Sit."

Eben glanced over at Lucy. "Good morning, Lucy."

Lucy nodded, then placed milk on the table for Thad and poured coffee for the adults while Deborah dished out scrapple onto plates and handed them to Lucy to take to the table.

"This looks delicious," Eben said genuinely.

"Denki." His compliment warmed her inside. She prepared her scrapple differently than most, so it always pleased her when someone liked her method.

"How have you been adjusting to life here in Colorado, Lucy?" Eben asked as they tucked into the meal after the prayer.

Lucy swallowed a bite of food. "Very well, thank you. It's so beautiful here, and Deborah and Thad are good hosts." She grinned at Deborah. "I'm excited for my brother and his wife to arrive. I hope they will love it here as much as I do."

Deborah realized she would miss quiet talks with the younger woman when she left, though it surprised her at times just how little Lucy knew about preparing traditional Amish meals. Deborah had enjoyed showing Lucy the different recipes her Mamm taught her, sprinkling in a few *Dietsch* lessons.

Although Lucy didn't like to talk much about herself, Deborah learned that her brother's name was Isaac and his wife was Katie. Lucy expected them to arrive in the San Juan Valley in couple of weeks' time after they'd finalized the sale of their Milverton home.

"How could they not? It's beautiful here." Eben sought out Deborah across the table. She struggled to ignore the way her stomach fluttered when his gaze was on her.

Gött, although I do not fully understand Your will for my life, I am grateful for the life You provide. Grant me Your wisdom and guidance.

"Are you looking forward to your workday with Samuel?" Deborah asked.

"I am. I'm excited to knock down that wall. Unfortunately, the diner must close during the remodeling. It will be a hardship for Samuel and Gertie to be closed and paying for the renovations."

She nodded. "Ja, but the benefits will make it worth the loss of income. I'm sure they have savings to help them through this time."

"Mamm, can I go outside and play in the snow?" Thad asked with a hopeful expression Making snowmen was one of Thad's favorite things to do when the snow piled up.

While she hated saying no, Deborah hadn't been able to get the footprints out of her head. "I don't think it's a *gut* idea. Besides, it's almost time to leave for school."

Thad trudged to the sink and placed his plate inside before he headed to his room.

Lucy rose from the table and gathered the dishes. When Deborah started to help, Lucy shooed her away. "I can handle this. It's the least I can do."

"Denki, Lucy. We'd better hurry if we want to make it to school in time. There's fresh snow. It will be a slow walk."

Eben cleared his throat. "With everything going on, perhaps it's best if you take the buggy today."

Deborah's gaze latched onto his. If Eben was worried about the footprints, perhaps it would be best if they didn't walk. "All right. I will go hitch Bridget for the trip." She retrieved her cloak and traveling bonnet and put them on.

"Let me help you." Eben slid his arms into his jacket. Once she put on her warm boots, Deborah lit a lantern and they stepped outside.

She brushed a wisp of hair from her face, walking beside him. "Thad looks forward to seeing you these days." Why had she said that?

"I enjoy being with him as well. He's bright and inquisitive and reminds me a lot of myself at that age."

She detected a hint of regret in his tone. "You miss the plain life."

He stared ahead. "I do. It was a simpler time for me. My family was close. The community looked after each other. At the time, I couldn't imagine living anywhere else but there."

She placed her hand on his arm. "I'm sorry you had to leave." Although he'd never told her why his father had left the faith, she sensed something ugly lay hidden in his silence.

Deborah held the lantern while Eben opened the barn door. Together, they worked to harness Bridget, then led her out to the front of the house where Eben tied the reins to one of the porch posts.

"What are your plans for the day?" Deborah asked Lucy once they went back inside. She was a little concerned about her new friend being alone. But there was an air of . . . competence about Lucy. Somehow, Deborah felt that Lucy could take care of herself.

"Oh, don't you worry about me. I brought some crocheting with me. I'm not very good at it, so I could use the practice. And don't forget I'm preparing the evening meal. That could take a while."

Deborah managed to keep a straight face. "I remember. You have my recipe for the ham-and-noodle casserole?"

"I do. I just hope I don't make a mistake. I'm not very good at it."

Deborah patted her arm. "When I first learned to cook, I burned more than my fair share of food. This one is a simple recipe, one of the first I learned to do correctly."

Lucy leaned over and gave her a hug. "Denki. I'm happy I have you to teach me these things. Someday, if it is God's will, I will have a family of my own. I wouldn't want my poor husband to starve."

Deborah chuckled. "You will do fine, and I imagine your Mann will be happy with any meal you prepare, burned or not."

Lucy laughed. "I'm sure he'd appreciate it a lot more if it weren't burned."

Thad ran into the room. Snatching his coat from the peg, he shoved his arms into the garment.

"Ready to go?" Eben asked and Deborah nodded.

"Have a *gut* day," Lucy told them. "Did I say that correctly?"

Deborah beamed at her friend. "Ja, perfectly. And you have a *gut* day as well. And keep the doors locked."

Outside, she watched her son shuffle, skip, and run to make different marks in the snow. Oh, to be a child and not feel the cold as adults did! His footprints reminded her that she hadn't seen any that morning at the barn. Perhaps she'd let her imagination get the better of her and made more of the situation than was truly there.

"Everything okay?" Eben asked as she stepped up on the buggy.

She forced the worries aside and took a seat next to her son. "Ja, everything is *gut*."

The gentle concern she saw in Eben's eyes took her breath away. Feelings she'd believed lost to her since Peter's death threatened to overwhelm her. But no matter how her heart urged differently, she couldn't go there. Their differences were too much to overcome.

When Deborah pulled up in front of the school a few minutes later, Eben following at a discreet distance behind, Thad spotted his friend. "There's David!" He waved, then hopped down and raced toward the boy. Deborah shook the reins and Bridget started down the snow-covered street once more until she reached the community horse shed and pulled in. A few minutes later, after seeing to the horse, she was at the door of her shop. Eben waved from his car, which was parked in front of the diner.

"Thad's a good boy," Eben said, coming up on the steps behind her. "You've done a great job with him, Deborah. This past year couldn't have been easy."

She swallowed. "It wasn't. Peter's death was so sudden. One minute he was here and then—" She hated thinking about her husband's final moments.

Staring up at Eben, she was aware of how attractive he was. The cold whipped a ruddy color into his cheeks and somehow made his eyes both clearer and bluer.

He had been raised plain. Were the differences between them so great after all?

"I will see you and Thad later," he assured her.

Without looking at him, she murmured, "Have a good day," then slipped inside and closed the door.

From the window, she watched Eben walk back across the street to the diner. She turned away, her hands unsteady. She was behaving foolishly.

She had one more Kapp to finish, and then Faith Wengerd's wedding garments would all be complete. She believed Faith would be pleased when she picked them up later that day. It would be *gut* for the community to watch those two young people joined in marriage soon.

Once she finished the Kapp, Deborah gathered the remaining garments and placed them into the box and closed the lid. Her obligations were done for today—although some customers would be nice.

She made herself a cup of Kaffe and glanced out the window behind the shop.

A man stood at the edge of the woods, his face contorted in anger as he stared at her shop.

Her heart leapt to her throat, and she quickly locked the back door with her pulse echoing in her ears. The door handle jiggled. He must have run from the woods and was now trying to get in! If she ran out the front door, would she be able to escape before he caught her?

Suddenly, the jiggling stopped, and she heard what sounded like footsteps running away.

Someone yelled. Eben! She unlocked the door in time to see Eben racing through the woods behind the shop after the strange man.

Eben disappeared from sight and she worried that the man might hurt him. There had been so much anger in his eyes.

As she continued to squint through the dense trees, Eben came back into sight. She hurried out to meet him, thankful that he was safe. "Are you oke?" she asked, resisting the urge to throw her arms around him.

Eben clasped her hands. "I'm fine. What happened?"

Getting words to come out seemed impossible. All she was aware of was how strong his hands felt wrapped around hers. She knew she was treading on dangerous ground—and anyone could see them. She stepped back and tried to calm her racing heart.

"I-I'm not really sure. I glanced up and saw him watching me from the woods. He looked angry. I locked the back door just in time. Eben, he tried to break in. Why would he do that?" She still couldn't believe what had happened.

"Have you seen him before?"

Deborah wrapped her arms around her body. "I don't think so." She glanced up at him, her eyes wide. "What about Thad?"

"I'm sure he's fine at school, but I'll go check on him. Stay inside and lock the doors. Don't open them until I return."

He walked her back to the shop and waited until she'd relocked it. Through the window, she saw him striding toward the school with purpose. She leaned against the locked door and closed her eyes, but she couldn't shut out the man whose furious glare seemed to bore right through her.

Eben eased toward the school, glad of the service weapon in his jacket pocket. He peered in the window where the children worked on their lessons. The teacher stood at the head of the class. There was no sign of the man. Eben caught the teacher's attention and motioned her to the door.

"May I help you?" she asked, startled by his sudden appearance.

"I need you to keep the children inside today. There's been someone wandering around the community. Until we know what he's up to, it's best to keep the Kinner out of sight."

The young woman's eyes widened. "Ja, I will keep them inside, but for how long?"

"For the rest of the day, just to be safe."

"Oke, I will keep them inside." She glanced behind her. "I'd best go back inside before they become too curious."

Eben headed back to the shop. He'd only caught a glimpse of the man's back, but he was positive it was Benson. There was no sign of him right now, but they'd need to make different arrangements from here on out. Eben couldn't afford to leave Deborah alone for a single minute, which meant Lucy would need to watch over her while she worked. They'd figure out how keep an eye on Thad too.

He knocked on the back window.

Deborah opened the window, the confusion in her eyes much less than the fear. He hated seeing such an ugly emotion on her gorgeous face.

"Thad is fine. I've asked his teacher to keep the kids in the classroom today. I'm going to have a quick look around. Keep the door locked until I return."

She nodded and closed the window again.

Once he reached a safe distance from the shop, he grabbed his cell phone and called his commander to let him know what happened.

"It sounds like Benson is making his move," Brian said, then hesitated, assuring Eben something else had happened.

"What is it?" Eben asked, dreading Brian's answer.

"I've had agents quietly searching for Henry Yoder for days now. It's as if he's dropped off the face of the earth. I don't like it, Eben. There's been no sign of him anywhere. The agents have been sitting on his house in the community as well as his previous home. I'm worried Benson may have harmed him."

Eben blew out a breath. "I'm inclined to agree. I'll get in touch with Lucy after we hang up. Have her keep an eye on Deborah during the workday. She can help with Thad as well."

"Good. Keep her and the boy close. I don't have to tell you how dangerous this guy is."

Eben ended the call, then texted Lucy to let her know what had happened and ask her to join Deborah at the shop today and for the foreseeable future.

Lucy replied almost immediately, confirming that she was on her way. As he started back toward the shop, Eben couldn't get what Brian had said out of his mind. His gut told him Yoder hadn't vanished of his own free will. Benson was involved somehow, but without a shred of evidence, tying Benson to the man's disappearance would be next to impossible.

6

Someone knocked on the door. Deborah glanced up from her sewing—she'd decided to start on a new project to keep her mind and hands busy—to see Lucy standing at the window, waving.

Laying down the garment she was working on, Deborah hurried to let Lucy inside. "Is something wrong?" she asked when she relocked the door. All she could think about was the angry man she'd seen watching her.

Lucy smiled. "Nay, nothing is wrong. I just got bored and decided to come in for a visit. I might as well get to know my new community. In fact, if you're okay with it, I would like to come to work with you each day. I think a shop is the best place to meet the people who live here."

"What a *gut* idea." Deborah would be deeply grateful for some company. She couldn't get the image of that man's burning eyes out of her head.

"Is everything okay?" Lucy asked, no doubt seeing Deborah's unease.

"It is not." With a sigh, Deborah told her about the man in the woods.

"Oh my! What do you think this man wants?"

Deborah wished she knew the answer to that question.

"Well now that I'm here, I am sure he won't try anything more. Would you show me around your shop?" Lucy asked, glancing around.

Deborah prayed Lucy was right. While there had been no further sighting of the man, she didn't believe he'd left the area. He would be lurking somewhere close by, waiting for another chance to get to her. She just wished she knew why.

"Ja, I would be happy to show you the shop." Deborah did her best to let go of her fears as she told Lucy about the history of the shop while they moved around it.

"It is wonderful," Lucy said at the end of the tour. "If you are okay with it, I would like to help out here each day. I know how to wash windows and sweep. Perhaps I can even do a little sewing." Lucy's eyes sparkled with anticipation.

"That is not necessary. I am happy just to have your company."

Lucy waved her hands in front of her. "I want to be useful. It will be fun, the two of us working together."

Deborah squeezed her arm. "Ja, it will be." In such a short time, her friendship with Lucy had become important to her, and Deborah couldn't imagine the day when her new friend would move out to live with her brother and sister-in-law, and then into a home of her own. At least she would still be nearby and they could see each other often.

"Why don't I start by sweeping up the showroom? When I'm finished, I can wash the inside windows." Lucy grabbed the broom from the corner and started sweeping with enthusiasm, sometimes pretending to dance around the room. Deborah chuckled at the sight. Lucy was funny and sweet and a hard worker. Still, she worried about the young woman's homemaking skills. Though Lucy rarely talked about her life in Canada and Deborah didn't pry, she grew curious about Lucy's Mamm. Why hadn't she taught her daughter how to keep a home and family?

Whatever the reasons were, they were none of her business. It was her business to teach Lucy, and she was glad to do it.

She opened the pattern Mrs. Henderson had selected and pinned the first piece to the material before carefully cutting it out. The elderly Englisch lady had purchased many dresses from Deborah. This time, she wanted two—a Christmas dress to wear to her church service, and a suitable dress for her granddaughter's wedding in the spring.

With the first piece of the pattern finished, Deborah smoothed out the material for the next. She noticed Lucy leaning the broom against the wall.

"I'm going to step outside to get some fresh air for a bit. I'll be back soon. Don't worry, I'll be careful," Lucy assured her when she spotted Deborah's worried frown.

"Oke." Letting go of her fears was not easy, but she would put her trust in Gött to protect both herself and her friend.

Once Lucy slipped outdoors, Deborah cut out the next piece of the pattern. Her gaze kept sliding back to the door. All she could think about was the anger engraved on the man's face. What did he want with her?

She straightened and glanced out the back window. Lucy was talking with Eben, waving her hands as she spoke. This was the second time Deborah had spotted them alone together. The night before, Lucy had followed Eben outside, and Deborah couldn't help but peek at them from behind the curtain. They seemed to be developing a personal connection.

As she watched, Lucy touched Eben's arm. Deborah looked away. Was there something going on between them? Seeing Eben with Lucy hurt, and she didn't understand why. She had no right to feel this way. Eben was no longer Amish. Neither she nor Lucy had any right to expect more from him than friendship. When Lucy headed back inside, Deborah hurried through to the shop and the cutting table.

She didn't want Lucy to think she was spying on her.

"It's snowing again," Lucy announced as she closed the door and locked it, shaking off the light dusting from her cloak.

"You must be used to the snow," Deborah said and tried to let go of her hurt.

Lucy took up the broom once more. "What do you mean?"

Deborah looked up from her cutting. "Coming from Canada. You must get lots of snow there."

"Oh . . . of course. I just didn't expect there to be so much here." Lucy did another little dance with the broom, but, for Deborah, some of the joy of the day had disappeared. All she could think about was Lucy and Eben together.

As the day went on, her hurt turned to anger. Was Eben deliberately leading both her and Lucy on? Deborah was old enough to know better, but Lucy was younger. In the future, Deborah would do her best to watch out for her friend. It wouldn't do for someone to see Lucy and Eben together and get the wrong idea. Against her will, she wondered what people must be thinking about her relationship with Eben. They'd spent quite a bit of time together.

Being former Amish, Eben should know he shouldn't be encouraging either woman. A relationship with him would be forbidden by the bishop. A sharp point of anger niggled at her.

After she'd finished cutting out the final piece for the dress, Deborah put away the pieces and brought out the basket she'd packed for lunch. "Are you ready to eat?" she asked. "I've brought plenty."

Lucy turned a smile her way. "Ja, I'm starving." She finished washing the window she'd been working on while Deborah cut thick slices of bread, then brought out the tuna salad she'd made that morning, which consisted of cream cheese, mayonnaise, lemon juice, and tuna along with chopped olives and black pepper. The recipe had been one of

Peter's favorites. She'd also brought along her canned bread-and-butter pickles and some homemade potato chips.

"This looks *wunderbaar*," Lucy exclaimed, repeating another word she'd learned, before sneaking a chip.

Folding her hands in her lap and trying to silence her thoughts, Deborah prayed with all her heart for Gött to take her anger away. It went against everything she believed in, and she had no right to feel this way. Eben was her neighbor and nothing more.

When they raised their heads, Lucy took a bite of her sandwich and glanced around. "I really do love your shop," she said, wiping her hand on her napkin. "It must be nice to be able to create such beautiful things."

"Denki," Deborah murmured without looking at her friend. She knew she was being childish, but she couldn't seem to help it.

"Is something troubling you?" Lucy asked when the silence between them stretched on.

Putting down her sandwich, Deborah chose her words carefully. "I consider you my friend, Lucy," she began.

Lucy's eyes became guarded. "Ja, I consider you my friend as well."

"Then as your friend, I feel I must warn you. Eben is not Amish. Any relationship you might imagine happening between him and yourself would not be allowed by the bishop."

Deborah waited for Lucy to say something, praying she hadn't overstepped.

Lucy clasped her hand, a gentle smile playing across her face. "Nothing is going on between me and Eben. I just happened to run into him outside. Besides, I have a boyfriend."

"You do?" Deborah asked, surprised by Lucy's use of the Englisch word *boyfriend*. Perhaps she had picked it up while she was on her Rumspringa. "Back in Milverton?" she asked, and wondered if the young man in question planned to move to their community once Lucy settled in.

"Ja, something like that." Lucy pulled her hand away and focused on her sandwich. Something about Lucy's story wasn't right. Deborah didn't pry, but she suspected Lucy might be running away from something.

"Well, *gut*. I just don't want to see you hurt. Eben is an attractive man, but he is not one of us."

A grin formed on Lucy's lips. "I am grateful for your concern, but you don't have to worry about me. I am happy to stay in your home and learn how to prepare your delicious meals. By the time my brother and sister-in-law arrive, they will be so surprised at how good I've gotten. I will make them your ham-and-noodle casserole. By the way, it's mixed up and ready to bake when we get home."

Deborah forced a smile. Lucy must have been spoiled at home if she never learned the basics of cooking. At her age, Deborah had been married and keeping house.

Once they finished eating, Deborah gathered up the leftovers and placed them back in the basket. As she glanced out the front of the shop, she shivered as she thought about the angry man again. Was he the same person who had been at her house? Who else could it be? The thought was chilling.

"I'll finish washing the windows, and then perhaps tomorrow you can show me how to make a dress," Lucy said.

Deborah enjoyed having Lucy around, and the feeling was even stronger now that they'd cleared the air. "Of course. You can help me with Mrs. Henderson's dress. It's a simple pattern."

"Simple is *gut*. I can handle simple." Lucy laughed, then gathered her cleaning supplies again.

Deborah decided to start on the skirt next. It was pleated and so the measurements and construction would need to be precise in order to look right. Then perhaps tomorrow she would show Lucy how to stitch up the sleeves.

She carried the pieces of the skirt to the sewing machine she'd set up near the front windows and set to work. In the distance, the mountains rose as a constant reminder of the unchanging love of Gött. Through all the heartache of the past year—the ache of losing Peter—Deborah had never once questioned Gött's purpose for her life.

Someone jiggled the handle on the front door and Deborah jumped to her feet and peered out the window, her heart racing. Martha Fisher stood at the door, a surprised look on her face. Deborah quickly unlocked it, and the woman stepped inside and closed out the brisk wind.

"I am sorry, Martha, I must have forgotten to unlock the door," she said by way of explanation.

"That is oke," Martha beamed. "How are you doing on this cold day?"

Deborah knew the older woman well and hugged her. "I am *gut*. The day is a beautiful one, ain't so?"

"That it is. But cold." Martha shivered to make her point, then glanced past Deborah to where Lucy stood. "And this must be your houseguest."

News spread quickly around the small community. "It is. This is Lucy Miller from Canada. She will be staying with me until her brother and sister-in-law arrive."

Martha beamed at Lucy. "How nice."

Lucy stepped forward and held out her hand. "It is nice to meet you."

Martha shook it warmly. "And you as well. Always *gut* to have young people come into our community. They bring so much life with them."

"They do," Deborah agreed. "What brings you to the shop today?"

"Ach, I want to make a quilt for my granddaughter, and I have a particular pattern in mind. I just need to find the right fabric."

"I'm sure we can find something to suit you. What design did you choose?" Deborah asked, leading the way to the rows of quilting fabrics.

"The Broken Star pattern. I have some nice cream material for the main part of the quilt, but I need some colors for the border and the star itself."

Deborah considered the materials. "Sarah is not quite a teenager, ain't so? Perhaps some of these purples would suit her. I think this combination would coordinate well, or maybe this one." She showed Martha several bolts of printed fabrics.

"Oh, these are quite lovely, Deborah. It will be hard to decide. Perhaps your young friend can help us out?" Martha turned to Lucy, who had followed them to the materials. Deborah silently blessed the older woman for making sure Lucy felt included.

Lucy beamed. "I'm happy to help." She examined the fabrics for a moment while Martha watched her as if the fate of the world were in her hands. "They are all pretty, but I think these two are my favorites." She selected two of Deborah's favorites as well.

Martha examined the fabrics, then nodded. "Ja, I agree with Lucy. These are fine colors. I will take them both."

Lucy appeared relieved. "Denki, Martha. I'm happy you agree."

Deborah took the two bolts to the table and cut the amount Martha requested. "If you need more, let me know."

"You know I'll be back." Martha glanced around. "What lovely quilts you have on display. I recognize Eva Nissley's work." Martha headed toward the quilt and touched it lovingly. "She is so talented. She and I were at school together, you know. We used to quilt with each other all the time back then. I never became as good as she is, though. I don't have her eye for patterns and colors."

Deborah certainly understood. "I would love to be able to make those beautiful quilts like you and Eva make. My Mamm taught me, but I'm not able to quilt like she did either. It is a true gift from Gött."

"That it is." Martha took her purchase and placed it inside her quilted bag. She moved to leave and then spotted the dress Deborah had begun. "Oh, another beautiful dress. You have your own gift, Deborah."

"Denki." Deborah smiled at the compliment.

"You are welcome." Martha glanced outside. "Well, I should be on my way. Joseph will be wondering what is taking so long. I will see you at the service on Sunday." With a final wave, she opened the door and stepped out into the afternoon.

"You made a *gut* choice on the materials," Deborah said to Lucy without facing her. When there was no answer, she spun around to find Lucy no longer stood close by. She found the girl staring out the workroom window. "Lucy?"

"Hmm?" Lucy seemed distracted.

"I said you made a *gut* selection," Deborah repeated.

Lucy smiled, but seemed to have other things on her mind. "Denki."

As the afternoon went on, Deborah's anxiety level continued to grow. She was grateful for the handful of visitors to the shop. They helped to take her mind off the thought of going home. What if the man from the woods was waiting there for her?

"I'm all done with the windows," Lucy said, startling her. "I think I'll take a quick stroll around town. Shall I collect Thad from school on my way back?"

"Thank you," Deborah said, and Lucy left through the back door.

Lucy appeared troubled. Deborah hoped it wasn't their earlier conversation.

Deborah went over to the window and scanned the area outside, but Lucy was nowhere in sight. Where had she gone?

With a shake of her head, Deborah returned to her work but found it hard to concentrate. She made a number of uneven, crooked stitches before she finally gave up and put the skirt away. Shadows lengthened outside. She would finish the skirt the tomorrow.

Glancing at the clock she kept behind the counter, she saw it was time to close anyway. She switched the sign on the door to *Closed*, then locked the front door.

From the back of the shop, voices drifted her way. Lucy was speaking with someone. She couldn't make out what Lucy said, but she recognized the second voice too. Eben. She braced herself to face him again. Sure, Lucy had assured her there was nothing between them, but what if Eben didn't feel the same way? Was he considering rejoining the faith for Lucy?

Darkness swelled in her heart.

Thad rushed into the room, followed by Lucy, then Eben. "Mamm, guess what? Lucy picked me up from school today!"

Deborah listened as he told her about how he and Lucy built a snowman behind the school.

"That's wunderbaar," she murmured, unable to look at Eben. She had no right to feel this way. It had been wrong to spend so much time with him, to have gotten so close. She must put some physical and mental distance between them.

"And then, when we were almost to the shop, Eben was waiting for us by the back door. He threw a huge snowball at us." Thad laughed. "But I got him back."

"*Gut* for you," she said, forcing a smile. She turned to gather her things.

"How was your day?" Eben asked her.

"Fine," she said, hoping her tone made it clear that she didn't wish to discuss it further. "Come, Thad, we must head home now. I want to check on the chickens before dark." A made-up excuse, but it was hard to be close to Eben and resist the urge to ask him about Lucy.

"I'll follow you," Eben said.

"That won't be necessary." Once she, Thad, and Lucy were seated in the buggy, Deborah urged Bridget toward home.

While Thad chatted about something he and David had done at school, Deborah barely heard what her son said. She'd been foolish letting herself imagine there could be something more than friendship between herself and Eben. Though painful, today's lesson was one she would not soon forget.

He followed them anyway.

When they reached the house, he parked and exited the vehicle. It was as if a wall had formed between him and Deborah and he didn't know why.

Or did he? He was Englisch now. There could be nothing between them.

When Lucy went to pick up Thad, she had texted him. Eben had stationed himself at the back door. There had been no further sightings of Benson today—at least, that he knew about.

He surveyed the house and barn. Nothing appeared out of place from where he stood, but Eben was worried about Benson. He extended his hand toward Deborah in the buggy. She ignored it and jumped down.

Lucy shrugged when he threw her a questioning look.

"Well, I should be going," he said. "I still have a few things around the house to finish up tonight."

"Good night, then," Deborah said and led the mare toward the barn without looking at him.

"But aren't you staying for dinner?" Thad asked hopefully.

Deborah whirled to face Eben, the stony look in her eyes giving him a clear answer.

"Not tonight, Thad," he said, and patted the boy's shoulder. "I'll see you tomorrow, though." He turned from Thad's disappointed face, got into the car, and headed to his temporary home.

Twilight had settled around the countryside as he drove. Had they been wrong? Perhaps Benson's interest didn't lie with Deborah or Thad as they'd believed. Maybe he'd gotten what he came for, namely Henry Yoder. But if that was the case, why had Benson tried to break into Deborah's shop that morning?

Once a safe distance from Deborah's house, he pulled over and called Brian again.

"Anything wrong?" Brian asked right away.

"No. Things have been quiet here since the incident at the shop. I don't mind telling you, Brian, I don't like it."

"Me either. Benson's still out there somewhere. I don't believe for a minute that he's abandoned his threat."

Eben felt the same way. "Any word on Yoder?"

Brian's deep sigh assured him the man's future looked grim. "I'm afraid not. Either he's on the run or something's happened to him."

"I agree. I spoke to Samuel Wyse earlier about Yoder, and he said Henry used to come into the diner every day for breakfast, but he hasn't seen him in a few days. During a break, I searched Yoder's house, but I didn't find any signs of a struggle. It's as if he simply disappeared. I don't like it."

"Me either. Keep your eyes open and stay on your toes."

After ending the call, Eben drove on to his house. Once inside, he grabbed the lantern off the kitchen table and lit it. The warmth of the morning's fire was long gone so Eben quickly built a new one.

His thoughts returned to Deborah. It gave him some comfort to know that Lucy was there with her and Thad, keeping them safe. But he couldn't help wishing he was there personally. He . . . missed her. And that was wrong on so many levels.

Stretching the kinks from his back, Eben opened the propane-powered refrigerator and took out the leftovers Deborah had sent home with him from their dinner the day before. Even though the casserole was cold, it was still delicious. Everything about the simple Amish recipes tasted so much better than the meals he was used to grabbing on his way home after long hours at the office back in DC.

Maybe because *everything* about this life felt like home to him.

He washed the bowl, resolving to return it to her the next morning and perhaps find a way to get her to talk to him. Turning from the sink, he glanced around at the cozy house. He was proud of the work he'd done in the kitchen, like the cabinets he'd repaired and the plumbing he'd gotten to operate. He believed his grandfather would be pleased with him.

Working at the old farmhouse was proving therapeutic. Though the place was only a rental, and technically it wasn't his job to make repairs, his accomplishments so far made it feel like a home. More and more, Eben envisioned living here in the San Juan Valley once the case ended. The things he'd seen as an FBI agent had branded themselves on his heart, wearing down his faith. Doing simple things like expanding a wall or replacing a cabinet hinge brought him much-needed peace.

And there was a certain woman with eyes that pierced his soul whom he was beginning to struggle to imagine living without.

7

After tossing and turning most of the night, Deborah finally abandoned sleep altogether and slid out of bed, the floor cold on her bare feet. Slipping on her dress, she carefully fastened her apron and cape in place with straight pins, then twisted her hair into a bun on top of her head and pinned her Kapp over it.

The door creaked as she opened it. Deborah held her breath, hoping not to wake the others. After a moment, she tiptoed to the kitchen and lit the cookstove. She struck a match to the lantern sitting on the table and carried it through to the great room.

Her Grossmammi's musical clock showed that it was barely four in the morning.

After stirring the embers in the woodstove, she added several logs to the fire, then went over to the desk in the corner and took out the Bible that had once belonged to her Grossdaddi.

In the front, the pages were filled with births, weddings, and deaths of family members. So many of her people had gone on to be with Gött.

Spending time with her grandparents was one of her favorite memories growing up. It saddened her that Thad would never know them. With her parents living so far away, she was grateful Peter's Daed and Mamm were close enough for him to see them each week.

Carrying the Bible into the kitchen, she made Kaffe—Lucy had told her she couldn't face the day without it—then opened the book to her favorite passages, letting the word of Gött soothe her troubled soul.

She'd behaved foolishly toward Eben without cause, and she

owed him an apology. No matter what might happen between him and Lucy, it was not her place to interfere. Gött had blessed her life with Thad, Peter's parents, and *gut* friends like Gertie and Samuel. Her community was there for support. She was in need of nothing and must be thankful for the time she'd had with Peter—and not go looking for the impossible.

With a sigh, Deborah closed the Bible and rose, removing sausage, eggs, and cheese from the refrigerator, planning to make a warm meal to start the day off right. After gathering a couple of potatoes from the pantry, she shredded them for hash browns, then put them on to fry.

"Something smells good." Deborah jumped at the sound of Lucy's voice and glanced over her shoulder. Lucy stood in the doorway, rubbing sleep from her eyes.

"Farmer's breakfast," she said, stirring the potatoes. "It's one of my favorites."

Lucy leaned over her shoulder. "I've never heard of it, but it looks wonderful, and I am hungry."

"You are always hungry," Deborah reminded her with a grin. Many of the recipes she loved to prepare had been passed down from her Grossmammi. Deborah was surprised that most of the traditional Amish recipes appeared new to Lucy. Maybe her home community had different foods.

Removing the potatoes from the skillet, Deborah crumbled sausage in to cook. "Do you mind stirring the sausage while I wake Thad? I won't be long." She handed Lucy the wooden spoon.

Lucy gazed warily at the pan. "Are you sure you trust me not to burn it?"

Deborah laughed at her friend's pained expression. "I trust you. You will do fine. Besides, I'll be back before you have time to burn it. But if you're concerned, pull it off the heat when there's no more pink, but before it turns black." She patted Lucy's arm and left the young woman standing over the stove with a doubtful look on her face.

Opening Thad's bedroom door, she went inside. Her son slept on his side facing away from the door as he had since he was tiny. Deborah sat on the bed and watched him for a while. So innocent, yet growing up more each day. A boy needed his father to teach him things she could not. Peter's Daed did his best, but Matthew was getting up in years and suffered terribly from arthritis. The cold weather made it difficult to do simple chores, much less teach an energetic boy how to do them.

Pushing aside her worries, she gently shook Thad. "Time to wake up," she whispered.

The boy scrubbed a hand across his eyes, then flipped onto his back and stared up at her, looking so much like his father that it took her aback for a moment.

"Come on, sleepyhead. Breakfast is almost ready." She smiled tenderly as he stretched, then threw back the covers and hopped out of bed.

"Can I help you feed the chickens today?" he asked.

She brushed hair back from his forehead. "We will see. Come, I left Lucy tending the sausage, and you know her cooking skills leave a lot to be desired."

Thad giggled. "Ja, she might burn the sausage."

Deborah joined in the amusement. They walked into the kitchen together where Lucy hovered over the skillet. Deborah winked at her son, and Thad laughed even harder.

"What's so funny?" Lucy whirled to get a good look at them.

"Nothing at all." Deborah managed to hide her amusement. "Do you want me to take over?"

The relief on Lucy's face made it hard not to burst out laughing. "Ja, please!" Lucy handed Deborah the spoon and passed by Thad, ruffling his hair. "How are you this morning, young Thad?"

"*Gut.* Did you burn our sausage?"

"Nay, I did not. I might turn out to be a cook after all," she said, a grin spreading across her face.

Deborah smiled to herself and finished the sausage. She added the potatoes back in, then scrambled eggs while Thad went about setting the table. While the eggs cooked, Deborah added cheddar cheese on top and let it melt before she placed the food on plates.

"Mamm, we can't eat until Eben gets here," Thad insisted, his sweet face screwed up in concern as they sat at the table.

Deborah shook her head. "Not this time. We are eating early. I will set a plate aside for Eben."

Though Thad wasn't happy with her decision, he tucked into his meal with a healthy appetite. When they'd finished, Deborah left Thad and Lucy to clear away the meal.

"I'm going to start the outside chores. I'll come get you when it is time to feed the chickens, oke?" she said, anticipating Thad's next question. "Help Lucy wash the dishes. I will be back soon." Taking up her cloak and bonnet, she lit the lantern and braced herself for the cold morning that greeted her.

Alert to her surroundings, she started toward the barn, trudging through the thick snowfall. Today, there were no new footprints out front. With all her heart she wanted to believe the things that had happened earlier were a mere misunderstanding. After all, who could have reason to be angry with her?

She lifted the wooden bar to unlatch the door when a noise nearby drew her attention away.

A man emerged from the woods. Her pulse exploded in her ears.

She recognized him. It was the man she'd seen watching the shop.

He stopped a few feet away, blocking her path to the house. "You are Peter Albrecht's widow."

Shock poured into her limbs. "How do you know about my husband?" The words came out as barely a whisper.

The man's mouth closed tight. Anger radiated from him like uncontrolled flames. "Because he took something that belongs to me, and I want it back." He stepped closer, pure evil in his eyes. "He must have given it to you. Where is it?"

Deborah stumbled backward. "I don't know what you're talking about." She tried to edge past the man, but he lunged to block her way and she fought back panic.

"What about Henry Yoder? Do you know him?" The question seemed even more surprising.

"Why do you want to know about Henry?" She forced the words out while her mind raced.

A muscle worked in the man's jaw. "Does he own other property around town besides his house?" he barked without answering her question.

Terrified, Deborah glanced past him to the house. "I don't know anything about Henry."

With an explosive growl, the man took another step closer, his eyes burrowing into hers. "You're lying. Perhaps someone else will remember where to find Yoder." He pivoted on his heel and headed straight for the house.

She screamed and ran after him, terrified for Thad's and Lucy's safety.

Before he reached the house, the front door flew open. Lucy stepped outside and shut the door.

"Go back inside," Deborah urged, worried the man would harm her friend.

But Lucy did no such thing. Deborah realized her friend was holding something—a gun.

The man spotted it at the same time she did. He whirled around and sprinted for the woods. Before Deborah had time to react, Lucy took off after him, her dark blue dress bunched around her knees, white Kapp strings blowing free behind her.

"Lucy, come back! He'll hurt you."

It was as if Lucy couldn't hear her. She charged deeper into the woods while Deborah tried to make sense of what was going on. Who was this man? What did he want with her? And why had Lucy brought a gun into her home?

She started up the steps when someone grabbed her from behind. Thinking the man had returned, she fought with all her might to free herself.

"Deborah, it's me," Eben said, turning her to face him. "What happened? Where's Lucy?"

She drew in a shaky breath and tried to reclaim her composure. She told him what had happened and how Lucy had chased after the man with a gun. As she spoke, one thing became frighteningly clear—Eben wasn't the least bit surprised by any of her shocking news.

"Let's get you inside where it's warm." Still holding onto her, he started for the house, but she wouldn't move.

"Lucy is in danger." She jerked her arm free, not understanding why he wasn't going after the young woman.

"She'll be fine. Come inside." The quiet urgency in his tone frightened her. Without another word, she hurried past him.

Seeing the fear on her son's face sent her rushing to Thad's side. She gathered him close. "It's oke. Everything will be okay," she soothed, feeling the boy's body quaking.

"Why did Lucy run after that man?" Thad gulped out the question.

Over the top of Thad's head, her gaze held Eben's. "I don't know."

Without offering an explanation, Eben headed for the door. "Stay here and lock the door. I'm going after Lucy." He left without waiting for her response.

With Thad clutching her hand, Deborah quickly locked the door, her mind brimming with questions.

"Is Lucy going to be okay?" Thad asked, his fearful eyes holding tears.

She tried to reassure him. "Ja, Eben will help her. We must trust Gött to protect her."

As she held her son close, her mind swirled with questions. Hours seemed to pass without any word from Eben or Lucy. All Deborah could think about was the anger on the man's face. What did he possibly think Peter had that belonged to him and why was he asking about Henry?

Finally, voices carried into the house, and she heard footfalls on the porch, followed by a knock. "Deborah, it's me," Eben said. Slowly untangling herself from Thad's arms, she unlocked the door and opened it. Eben stepped over the threshold with Lucy, the weapon no longer in sight.

Deborah latched onto Eben's gaze. Something bad was coming—she saw it in his eyes. "Thad, go to your room." Her voice sounded strained.

Thad's huge eyes shot around toward each of the adults, then he spun around and ran to his room.

When his door was closed, Deborah asked Lucy, "Why did you bring a gun into my home?" No scenario she could imagine would explain her friend's behavior.

"We have to tell her," Lucy told Eben. "She needs to know what she's facing."

Eben slowly nodded. "You're right." He turned to Deborah. "You'd better sit down. This won't be easy to hear."

She lifted her chin, dreading his answer. "Just say it." It felt as if her world were collapsing all over again.

"Lucy and I are FBI agents." He waited for her to absorb this. "We're here to find a man who is responsible for money laundering, and possibly a far greater crime. That man was the one you saw outside your house."

Her thoughts wouldn't come together. Everything she thought she knew about Eben and Lucy was a lie.

"This man, why is he following me and Thad? What does he want with us?" They were peaceful people. Violence went against everything the Amish believed in.

"He believes you have something that will tie him to your late husband's death. Something that can put him away for a very long time. He has to find it before we do."

Her brows shot up. What Eben said mirrored the man's words. "My husband's death? Peter fell from a roof he was working on. His passing was an accident." She wanted him to agree, but the solemn look on his face told her everything she'd believed about her husband's death was about to be proven wrong.

He took her hands, the tenderness on his face robbing her of breath. "We don't believe Peter's death was an accident. You see, your husband used to work for a man by the name of Victor Benson, the man you saw outside." He blew out a breath. "We think Peter may have witnessed something before his death that might incriminate Benson, and for that reason, Benson had to get rid of Peter." He paused a second. Dread settled around her. "Deborah, we believe Benson pushed your husband off the roof to silence him."

Her legs threatened to give out, and she wished she'd sat down when Eben suggested it. She could not bring her thoughts into focus. Peter was murdered? Her and Thad's lives were in danger?

She fought back tears. "So everything you've told me about yourself was a lie?" She lashed out at Eben. "Instead of making the Glicks' place a working farm, you are really hunting down this man." Deborah drew in an unsteady breath. "I trusted you and Lucy, and you both lied to me. I thought of you as a friend, as—" The words broke off, tears choking her voice. She bit her bottom lip hard. She would not cry in front of him.

All this time she thought she was getting to know Eben, but he had simply told her what she wanted to hear to do his job. He'd pretended to be someone he wasn't. He'd spent time with her as part of his work assignment.

She pulled her hands free and covered her mouth with a trembling hand. She'd behaved naively and brought this all on herself by trusting an Englischer. Opening her heart up to him. Never again.

"Deborah, I'm so sorry we had to keep you in the dark," Lucy told her. "We needed to protect you and Thad from Benson. He's a dangerous man."

Deborah could no longer look at either of them. All she could think about were the lies. "So that makes it oke to lie? You pretended to be my friend." She drew in a shaky breath. "I invited you into my home. Taught you how to cook and showed you my shop. I enjoyed the time we spent together, but you were just acting a part."

"That's not true. We *are* close," Lucy assured her. "It wasn't an act. I truly enjoy spending time with you."

Deborah couldn't help but feel betrayed. She'd thought Lucy was her friend, but it was all an act. She thought there was more between herself and Eben, a connection, as impossible as it was. She'd been wrong about that as well. How foolish she felt. "You should have told me the truth," she said to Lucy, then turned her anger on Eben. "You didn't have to pretend to be my friend. Why didn't you just tell me the truth?"

The hurt in Deborah's eyes shredded Eben's heart. He turned to Lucy. "Can you give us a minute?"

Glancing from Eben to Deborah, she nodded. "I'll take another look around outside. Maybe he left something behind that will help us find out where he's hiding."

Eben waited until the door closed. "I'm sorry I had to keep you in the dark. I never wanted to lie to you. We were afraid someone in the community might inadvertently tip Benson off to our presence here. The more people who know a secret, the harder it is to keep it."

She waved a hand at him. "I've heard enough. I need to check on my son." Without another word, she brushed past him, leaving him alone.

Running his fingers through his hair, Eben realized he'd made a rookie mistake. He should have kept his distance. Instead, he'd been drawn to her right from the beginning, graying the boundaries he needed to keep between them. For a while, he'd let himself believe it might be possible to return to his Amish roots, even to share them with her. Foolish.

The front door opened. Eben turned to see Lucy standing in the doorway, glancing around. "Where's Deborah?"

"With Thad." He squared his shoulders, ignoring the questions in her eyes. "Did you find anything useful?" He'd try to speak with Deborah later, once she calmed down. Perhaps she'd be willing to hear him out.

Lucy shook her head. "I tracked him to a large creek some distance away before his footprints disappeared. There was an engine noise fading in the distance. I think he used a snowmobile to escape.

Until we can get this guy, do you think it's safe for Deborah and the boy to be out in public?"

He heaved a weary sigh. "Probably not, but we don't want to let Benson know the FBI is onto him more than we already have. Showing Benson your gun put him on alert. Let's hope it didn't blow the operation entirely. It's too important. We need to catch this guy before he hurts someone else. Who knows what he's done to Henry Yoder?"

Lucy agreed. "I'll do another pass around the house and barn and meet you outside when they're ready to leave."

While he tried to decide the best plan for everyone, Deborah came back into the great room with Thad by her side, still terrified. That fear seemed to be much more than worry for Lucy's safety.

Eben knelt in front of the boy. "Thad, what's wrong?"

Thad shook his head, his eyes huge. He was too frightened to even talk. Eben suspected the boy knew more than he'd told them, but one glance at Deborah's face kept him from asking more questions.

"Go get your coat, Thad. It's time to leave for school." Deborah waited until the boy was out of earshot. "I do not wish for Thad to miss school, but is it safe for him to be there with this man still out there?"

Eben straightened and faced her. "Lucy and I will keep watch over you and Thad during the day. You will be safe."

She didn't appear convinced. "For how long? When will this end, Eben?"

Before he could answer, the noise of a buggy approaching could be heard coming down the path to the house. Thad returned and clung to his mother's side.

"It's oke." She stroked the hair from his face. Together they went over to the window and looked out. "It's Bishop Timothy."

"Were you expecting him?" Eben asked.

"No, but he sometimes stops in to visit. I will not keep this from him, Eben. It would be a sin. He must know what's happening in his community." She squared her shoulders, preparing for an argument.

She was right. Keeping information of this type from the bishop would make her guilty of lying. He couldn't let her face the bishop's judgment.

Without waiting for his answer, Deborah started outside with Thad clinging to her side. Dread slipped into the pit of Eben's stomach as he imagined the bishop's reaction. Would he order Eben and Lucy to leave the community immediately? No matter what the bishop's ruling, Eben wouldn't leave Deborah and Thad unprotected.

"Deborah, it is *gut* to see you." Bishop Timothy dismounted and came forward, a jovial smile on his face.

Before Deborah formed an answer, Lucy rounded the side of the house, stopping when she saw the bishop.

"And this must be your guest from Canada," the bishop continued warmly.

"Ja, this is Lucy," she said, with a worried glance Eben's way.

The bishop shook hands with Lucy, then noticed Eben. "You have another visitor?" Bishop Timothy arched a brow at the sight of Eben. "How are the repairs going?"

"Actually, that's something I need to talk to you about." Pulling in a breath, Eben told the bishop who they were and why they were there. When he'd finished, the stern expression on the bishop's face gave away his opinion.

"This is most disturbing news. To have law enforcement agents here in our peaceful community. I should have been told about your plans before you came." Anger blazed in his eyes. "Your presence here puts everyone in danger and brings disorder to our community. We

Amish do not condone violence. I must ask you and your partner to leave immediately." Bishop Timothy started toward his buggy. "And I will expect you to abide by my wishes."

Eben followed. "With all due respect, I'm afraid I can't do that. Deborah's and Thad's lives are in danger. I won't allow this man to hurt them."

Bishop Timothy whirled, his face flushed. "That is unacceptable. You bring your Englisch ways and crime into our lives. I ask you to respect my wishes and leave. The community will keep them safe."

"That's not an option. I'm sorry I was unable to tell you before, but we couldn't afford to tip Benson off that we were coming after him." Eben stepped to within a few feet of the bishop, not wanting Thad to overhear what he said next. "Benson slipped away once. We can't let that happen again. We believe he is responsible for taking Peter Albrecht's life."

Shock replaced the bishop's anger. "What do you mean, he is responsible?"

Eben glanced over to where Deborah stood. Pale as a sheet, she clutched Thad close. He couldn't imagine how hard this would be for her to relive the details of her husband's death. He took the bishop aside and told him everything they suspected of Benson. Once he'd finished, the bishop's anger returned.

"All the more reason why this should have been brought to my attention. It is my duty to look after the welfare of my community."

"I know, sir, and I am sorry about the secrecy," Eben told him sincerely. "But we can't leave, Bishop. I could not forgive myself if something were to happen to Deborah or Thad because I left my post. One of your community members is missing already. Henry Yoder has not been heard from in days. We believe something bad has happened to him at Benson's hands."

The elderly man sized Eben up without answer, then something akin to admiration shown in his eyes. "I will expect to speak to your superior today. I want to know why he ordered this to take place without first speaking with me and what the dangers are to this community." The bishop's stern tone brooked no argument. He climbed up on the seat and shook the reins, leaving them without another look.

Eben glanced at Deborah. "We should get going. We don't want Thad to be late for school." He headed up the steps of the house and held the door open for her.

She slipped past him without a glance.

As soon as he had an opportunity, he'd call Brian and let him know what had happened. With the task force set up in Alamosa, it shouldn't be a problem for Brian to meet with the bishop. Hopefully he could convince the man to allow them to remain.

Regret weighed heavy on Eben's shoulders. Alienating Bishop Timothy had never been his intention. It seemed all he had managed to do since arriving was create things to be sorry for.

8

Deborah looked around for Thad, but the boy had seemingly disappeared. Fear flooded her heart and she rushed to find him.

Thad lay curled up on his bed in his room.

"Thad, was iss letz? Are you sick?"

He stared up at her with huge tearful eyes.

She felt his forehead. It was cool to the touch, but the boy still would not speak.

She noticed Eben standing in the doorway. He motioned her outside and she slowly followed him, closing Thad's door.

"Do you think he overheard what I said about his Daed?" Eben asked.

Her heart clenched at the thought. "I don't think so."

Eben took a step closer. Somehow, she resisted the urge to retreat. He was a liar, and she was just his job. There was nothing to be afraid of from him. "I'm sorry you had to find out about us this way, but to be honest with you, I'm glad you know. I hated keeping this secret."

She did not share his relief. She'd trusted Eben, believed everything he'd told her. She'd even found herself wishing for more from their relationship than was possible.

"I just want this to end," she murmured, unable to keep the hurt from her tone.

Clasping her arms, he searched her face. "I realize this is hard, but you're safe. I'm not going to let anything happen to either of you."

She tore her gaze from his and freed herself from his grasp. "Perhaps I should keep Thad home today. This has been difficult for him."

"Would you allow me to speak with him? I promise I won't do anything to upset him further."

The last thing she wanted was to hurt Thad more, but she wanted to trust Eben, even after he'd proved she couldn't. She slowly nodded. "Oke."

He squeezed her shoulder. "Thank you." Stepping past her, he headed into Thad's room and Deborah followed.

Her son faced the wall, his back stiff.

"Thad, look at me," Eben said gently.

Slowly the boy rolled over, his face ravaged.

"I know what happened earlier was scary, but I want you to know you and your Mamm are safe. Do you believe me?"

The boy slowly nodded.

"Did you recognize the man from earlier?" Eben's question took Deborah by surprise. Why would he think Thad might know this man?

She studied her son's face. He did know.

Thad finally said, so quietly they almost didn't hear him, "He hurt Henry Yoder."

Eben shot her a glance, then asked, "How did he hurt Henry? When did this happen?"

Thad's bottom lip quivered. "When I left my coat in the woods." He glanced at Deborah. "Henry gave me the coat and asked me to take it home and put it somewhere safe, but I wanted to wear it because it reminds me of my Daed."

Deborah's heart went out to her son. She sat down on the bed and took his hand.

"What happened the day you left the coat in the woods?" Eben asked.

Tears spilled down Thad's face. "I saw Henry after David went home. Henry was angry with me for wearing the coat. He pulled it off of me because he wanted it back." The boy scrubbed his face. "Then we heard someone coming, and he shoved me and Daed's coat into the bushes. I peeked out and saw that man."

"The one Lucy and I chased this morning?" Eben asked.

Thad nodded. "He and Henry were shouting at each other. I think Henry knew him." Through tears, Thad said, "That man hit Henry with a big stick and he fell asleep." The words were barely audible. "Then the man dragged Henry away. I waited until he was out of sight, and then I ran as fast as I could to my Mamm's shop. I guess I forgot the coat." He hung his head.

Deborah could not believe the terror her child had endured. "Why didn't you tell me what happened?" she asked gently.

Tears rolled down Thad's cheeks. "I was scared you would be mad at me."

Deborah sat on the edge of the bed and gathered him close. "You did nothing wrong, so I have no reason to be mad at you." How could Henry know someone like Benson? Henry was a kind man who wouldn't hurt anyone.

"Thad, I'm going to step outdoors and have a word with your Mamm, and then we'll be right back." Eben stood and waited while Deborah kissed her son's forehead and pulled his arms from around her waist.

"I won't be long, I promise," she assured the boy before she followed him once more out of the room.

Eben motioned to the front door. He didn't want Thad to overhear their conversation.

Deborah put on her cloak and wrapped it tightly around her body. Stepping outside, she closed the door and faced him.

"What did you want to speak to me about?" she asked, her tone colder than the winter air around them.

Breaking through the new wall between them seemed an impossible feat. "I think you should know everything about Victor Benson's connection to your community."

She clutched her cloak tight, a troubled expression on her face. "How could this man be connected to our community?"

"Because Benson has a string of shops across Colorado. He sells products that are made here in the San Juan Valley along with other Amish communities. I'm sure he's acquainted with several local people. That's why we were afraid someone might tell him we're here. He's a dangerous man, Deborah. His businesses are fronts for money laundering for an organized crime syndicate that operates here in Colorado."

Surprise gleamed in her eyes. Did she believe him?

"Benson's proven he will stop at nothing to protect himself and his business partners. Even if it means murdering someone. Every minute Henry is unaccounted for, his life is in danger. We have to find him before it's too late."

Her eyes widened. "How can I help?"

He'd promised her the truth. Going back on his word now would destroy their relationship. "There's something you should know. Henry Yoder isn't his real name. He's really an Englischer named Ed Zachary. He was supposed to help the FBI convict Benson of money laundering until he disappeared shortly after Peter's death. At the time, we feared Benson had got to him, until we discovered he'd taken up residence here."

Those beautiful, fearful green eyes bore into him. All he could think about was how he wanted to take her in his arms and hold her close, tell her that everything would be okay. Yet she wasn't his to hold. And he couldn't make that promise when he had no idea if they could stop Benson.

"That man—he mentioned Henry by name," she said softly.

He couldn't believe what she said. "What do you mean? He spoke to you?"

She managed a tiny nod. "Ja. He wanted to know if Henry owned any property around town besides his house."

Benson's question threw him. Was it possible Henry had managed to escape from Benson? "Did he say anything else?"

"He asked if Peter left me anything important." She rubbed her arms, shivering. The haunted look in her eyes worried him.

Without thinking, he gave in to his desire and gathered her close. "Hey, it's going to be okay. I won't let him hurt you or Thad. My commander will speak with the bishop. We'll make this right, I promise."

Against his chest, she shook her head, then stepped back. "No, you do not understand."

"What don't I understand?"

For the longest time, she didn't say a word, clearly trying to decide whether to tell him something. Meanwhile all sorts of disturbing thoughts raced through his head.

"Please just tell me," he urged.

She drew in a breath. "The day Peter fell from the roof, he wasn't alone."

Dread settled over him like a thundercloud waiting to rain down on them. "What do you mean, he wasn't alone?"

"My husband and Thad were so close," she said, almost to herself.

"They did everything together. Thad spent every possible moment in Peter's company." Deborah peered deep into his eyes. "On the day Peter fell, he wasn't alone. Thad had gone to work with him. Eben, my son witnessed his father's murder."

9

His eyes widened with her news. "He must have seen Benson push your husband. Do you understand what this means? Thad is a witness. He can help us put Benson away for a very long time. This is good news."

Good news? She didn't see it that way. Her son had witnessed his father's murder. For a year, she'd had no idea the extent of his suffering. Watching his Daed slip was bad enough, but watching someone kill the most important man in his life? Would Eben expect Thad to bear witness against Benson? The idea of her sweet son having to relive those horrific moments tore at her heart.

"I will not force Thad to tell what he saw that day. It's too much to ask." She'd fight Eben and anyone else who tried to push the issue.

Eben clasped her arms. "Let's not get ahead of ourselves. We don't know for sure what Thad witnessed. Did he mention seeing his Daed's fall?"

In the past, in spite of all her coaxing, Thad had refused to speak of that day. She finally understood why. "It doesn't matter what he saw. I don't want him questioned about this. He's been through enough just losing his Daed." She shifted away. "Now, knowing he might have witnessed this man harm his Daed—it's too much."

He gently turned her face toward him. "I know this is hard, but I'm asking you to please trust me. I'm not going to put Thad in a situation that would be harmful to him, and his testimony could protect a lot of people, including you and himself."

The sincerity she saw in him made her want to believe. "Oke," she whispered at last and prayed she'd made the right choice. Warmth swept over her as he continued gazing at her with such tenderness. Her eyes closed. Drawing a steady breath was suddenly impossible.

"Deborah," he whispered.

She swallowed and stepped back, struggling to find calm. An awkward silence settled between them.

"You're right," he said at last. "Thad should stay home today. After what happened, I don't want him or you out in the open until we can figure out what Benson was after."

His words did little to calm her fears. "What if he comes back? If Thad did witness this man kill his father, then he will keep coming after him. You and Lucy can't stay here forever. What happens once you leave?"

"I'm not going anywhere, Deborah," he said without hesitation, and hope took flight in her heart. She forced it down. She should not wish for what could not be.

"You mean until Benson is caught," she finished for him.

Moving closer, the expression on his face swept her breath away. "I mean for as long as I'm needed," he said softly, sending a shiver up her spine. "In the future, I think it best if I stay here for added protection. I can bunk down in the barn. It'll be cold, but I've slept in colder places. With my sleeping bag and some extra quilts, I'll be comfortable enough."

She didn't know what to say, but he didn't seem to expect a response. "I'll go have a word with Lucy first and let her know we're staying home, then I'll go get my belongings. I'll need to speak with my commander and take care of some things, but I should be home before supper.

Home. She liked the way he said the word a little too much. It promised things unattainable. Without answering, she turned on her heel and went back inside. Closing the door behind her, Deborah leaned against it, her heart thundering against her chest. She had always felt so safe in this house, but now that safety was threatened.

Deborah peeked in on Thad and found the boy fast asleep, probably worn out from the terror and grief of the morning. Tiptoeing to the bed, she covered him with the quilt her Mamm had made. Thad was her life. That he'd suffered so much this past year ripped her heart apart. Leaning over, she kissed his forehead. With one final glance, she left the door open a crack in case he got scared, and she returned to the great room. The chill of the day seeped down deep. Stoking the fire, she sank into one of the rockers.

Knowing Eben had lied to her hurt more than she could have imagined. Everything he'd told her about his life was called into question. Had he really ever been Amish? Tears stung her eyes. She blinked them away when the door opened and Lucy came inside.

Even though they hadn't known each other for long, the friendship Deborah thought they'd formed seemed real. As an only child growing up, she always wanted a little sister. With Lucy, it almost felt as if she'd found one.

"I'm sorry," Lucy said, barely loud enough to hear. She slipped into the rocker next to Deborah.

"I just wish you had been honest with me from the beginning. I thought we were becoming friends. Now . . ." She lifted her shoulders.

"We *are* friends. And I really hate that I couldn't tell you the truth in the beginning." Lucy touched her hand. "It wasn't an act for me. I really do consider you a friend."

"I guess now I know why you can't cook." Deborah managed a smile.

Lucy's brow shot up, then she burst out laughing. "I knew I wasn't fooling you with my 'I never learned to cook' excuse."

"You almost did. Most Amish girls are taught how to cook at a young age. I thought your parents must have spoiled you terribly."

"They did, just not in the way you thought," Lucy said. "But I've learned so much from you these past few days. Before, I never really enjoyed cooking. Now, I'm actually proud of what I've done. And I hope we can continue with our lessons while I'm here."

Deborah squeezed her hand. "Do you really have a brother?"

Lucy shook her head. "I'm an only child. That's something we have in common. I truly have enjoyed learning about the Amish way of life. I'm going to miss it when this case ends."

Deborah couldn't imagine the type of life Lucy lived. Deborah's life here in the San Juan Valley was blessed with peace and a community where people looked out for one another.

"*Gut*, then you can help me milk the cow and finish the morning chores."

Lucy stared at her wide-eyed. "You're kidding."

Deborah shook her head and rose. "Nay. It's time you learned how. Come with me please."

He'd hurt her badly. Even though they'd only known each other a short time, he'd come to care for her and Thad. He'd fought against these feelings, but they were impossible to deny.

And now he'd hurt her.

Gathering the things he'd need for an extended stay, Eben hauled them out to the car, then called Brian and let him know about Bishop Timothy's demand.

Brian sighed. "It appears you were right all along. We should have cleared this with the bishop. I'm sorry I didn't listen to you, Eben. I just thought the fewer people who knew what was happening the better."

"We have a chance to make things right now. We need the bishop's support."

"I agree. I can be there in two hours. I'll meet you at the bishop's home on the edge of town."

"Sounds good. I'll see you then." Eben ended the call and drove into town. He had something to do before meeting Brian. There'd been enough lies. Samuel and Gertie deserved the truth too, and he knew he could trust them to keep his secret.

He parked in front of the diner. By now, Samuel would be worried. Eben normally arrived early in the morning and it was almost midday. He stepped inside the diner, grateful that with the expansion in progress, the restaurant remained closed. Normally, Gertie would be in the kitchen working. To keep money coming in, she baked pastries each morning and sold them at a restaurant in Alamosa.

With no one in sight, Eben went through to the expansion room where he found Samuel sawing a board. He glanced up as Eben approached, a smile creasing his face. "*Ach*, there you are, Eben. I was beginning to worry." His smile disappeared when he saw Eben's expression. "Something is wrong."

Eben nodded, aware of Gertie standing in the opening behind him. He told them the truth about being an FBI agent and Benson's threats against Deborah and Thad.

"*Mein Gött*," Gertie exclaimed, hurrying to her husband's side.

"This man is dangerous. He must be caught," Samuel said, his jaw set tight, anger staining his cheeks.

"He is and he will. I needed you both to know why I couldn't be here today. But I do want to continue the work whenever possible."

"You must take care of Deborah and Thad first," Samuel told him. "But you are a *gut* carpenter, Eben. I suspect you have done this type of work many times in the past."

Eben bowed his head. "I have."

Gertie placed a hand on his arm. "Your heart is troubled. Is there something we can do to help?"

Eben's face crumbled. He didn't deserve their kindness. He'd lied to them, to so many people in the name of justice.

"I think it's too late for me," he said, his smile twisted as bitterness entered his tone. He told them about his past, the desire of his heart to one day return to his Amish roots. Eben hadn't thought about it in a long time until he'd come here and met Deborah. She made him long for the plain life again.

"It is never too late for Gött," Gertie said softly. "He is the Father of second chances. Let Him help you find yours."

Eben wasn't so sure. He'd seen so much of the dark side of human nature. His past always lingered in the background to remind him he wasn't worthy to be called Amish anymore. "I hope you're right," he said. "I should go, but I hope to see you both soon."

Samuel clamped a hand on Eben's shoulder. "We *will* see you soon," Samuel corrected and Eben grinned at the typical Samuel remark, then left the couple he'd come to consider as his friends.

Eben stopped by the store and bought some locks and extra window latches for Deborah's home. He'd install them for added security. With time before meeting Brian, he took another look around Deborah's shop and the nearby woods. Nothing jumped out at him. Still, Benson was out there somewhere, waiting to strike again.

Driving out of town, he turned off on the gravel road that ran in front of Bishop Timothy's home. Brian had parked along the road near the drive. Eben stopped next to him and rolled the window down.

"I'll follow your lead since you've met the man and are familiar with the Amish customs."

Eben nodded, then put the car in gear, turning onto the drive.

Brian followed him to the house and pulled up next to Eben. Together, they mounted the steps to the porch. Eben knocked and waited as footsteps sounded from inside the house.

The bishop slowly opened the door and eyed both men without speaking.

"Bishop Timothy, this is my commander, Brian Anderson." Brian extended his hand. After a moment of hesitation, the bishop accepted it. "Would it be okay if we speak with you for a moment?"

The elderly man eventually nodded, opening the door to them. They followed him into a kitchen dominated by a wooden cookstove. A simple white cloth covered the table, a kerosene lamp sat in the center, and two wooden benches on either side.

Eben's steps faltered for a second. Everything about the room—this community—reminded him of the past he longed for more and more each day.

A woman around the same age as the bishop stirred something on the stove. Her eyes followed them as they entered the room, but her face remained impassive. The deep-blue color of her dress contrasted with her white apron. Tufts of salt-and-pepper hair in a traditional middle part peeked out from under her Kapp.

"My wife, Miriam." Bishop Timothy smiled gently at the woman.

"Nice to meet you," Eben and Brian said at the same time.

Miriam inclined her head without uttering a word.

"Please sit." The bishop pointed to the bench seats, and they did so while Miriam prepared coffee in a percolator on the stovetop.

"Now, tell me what is happening with this man you are after." Bishop Timothy thanked his wife for the coffee she placed in front of them. Still without a word, she left them alone.

At Brian's request, Eben told the bishop about their suspicions concerning Victor Benson. After what Deborah told him earlier, he was convinced Benson wished to harm Thad as well, but he kept the part about Thad witnessing his father's murder to himself. He'd promised Deborah.

"Bishop, I know having a police presence in the community goes against the Ordnung, but we can't let this man harm any more innocent people. As you know, we suspect he may have done something to Henry Yoder already."

Keen eyes reflected the bishop's concern. He stroked his white beard thoughtfully. "Henry is a *gut* man. Though new to our community, he is well respected by our members. After what you've told me, I am worried about him as well. Henry did not show up at the community dinner the other night, and no one has seen him lately. It is troubling."

Eben told him what Thad had said about Benson knocking Henry out and dragging him away. "As you can see, this man is dangerous and believes Deborah has something that will incriminate him."

The bishop held his gaze for the longest time before slowly nodding. "You must protect Deborah and Thad. I will allow you to remain in the community and I will quietly alert some of our members to be watchful of this man."

It was more than Eben had hoped for. "Thank you, Bishop. I'm sorry for the misunderstanding, but we were only trying to do what we believed to be safest for Deborah and Thad."

Bishop Timothy inclined his head. "I can see you are sincere, and I trust you will do right by them. Let me know when you find Henry."

Eben nodded and rose to his feet, knowing the dismissal when he heard it. "I will." They followed Bishop Timothy to the door, ready to leave.

"May I have a moment alone with you, young man?" Eben's brows shot up. Bishop Timothy's request came as a surprise.

"Of course." He turned to Brian. "I'll be right out."

Brian nodded to the bishop, then closed the door behind him.

Eben had no idea why the bishop wanted to speak with him alone. As he waited, his heart pounded in his chest. He felt unworthy to stand in this man's presence.

"I sense you are troubled," Bishop Timothy said quietly. "You were once Amish, am I right?"

Eben was floored that the bishop had guessed the truth. "Yes. My father was excommunicated when I was seventeen."

The bishop's keen eyes held his. "Your father chose not to repent?"

Eben forced words out. "That's right." He told the bishop about his father's sin.

"And your father never wanted to return to the faith?" The question took Eben by surprise. He thought about how his father followed the rules of Ordnung even though he was no longer Amish.

"I don't know. We've never talked about it." His voice cracked, the words barely audible.

"And you?" The man watched him, seeing things Eben could no longer deny.

"It's too late for me," he muttered, unable to look at the holy man.

"Is it? Your father's sins are not yours, Eben," the bishop said gently. "You were never baptized?"

Eben shook his head.

"Being back here has brought back feelings you have not dealt with. You must pray for Gött's wisdom. Let Him guide your decision."

The bishop from his former district had watched over the community with a firm hand. Bishop Timothy didn't seem to be anything like that man. He was kind and perceptive. He understood his people and wanted the best for them.

"I wouldn't know where to start."

The man smiled kindly and patted his arm. "I can help. When you are ready, come see me and we will talk about this more."

"Thank you, sir." His eyes brimming, Eben blindly grabbed the door and opened it. The door closed softly behind him, and he stopped to regain his composure.

Glancing back at the house, he noticed the bishop watching him from a window. Could he return to this life he so longed for? His heart felt lighter than it had in years.

"What was that about?" Brian asked when Eben joined him again.

Eben wasn't ready to talk about what he and the bishop discussed. "He had a few questions about my living arrangements at Deborah's home. I put his mind at ease."

Brian unlocked his car. "I'm heading back to the command center. We have men looking for Henry Yoder at some of Benson's old hangouts. Hopefully, he will turn up soon."

Unfortunately, the more time that passed, the less likely it was that they'd recover Henry alive.

With a final wave to Brian, Eben climbed into the car and left the bishop's property. By now, the sun was low in the sky, its soft light glinting off the snow-covered fields as he drove toward Deborah's farm. Night came early in the shadow of the mountains.

His thoughts wandered back over what Bishop Timothy said. Could it be possible to have a second chance at the life he'd once loved, or was he simply remembering the past differently?

Deborah's beautiful face came to mind. Her gentle smile as she teased him melted his heart. The way she cared for her son. The strength she possessed in spite of everything that had happened in her life reminded him of his Grossmammi. Like Deborah, she had been the heart of their family.

The house came into view and he tried to compartmentalize his feelings. Finding Benson had to be his top priority. Before Benson hurt anyone else.

Deborah, Lucy and Thad emerged from the barn as he pulled up. Deborah stooped to study something her son pointed out in the snow. The sight of them together reminded him of the plain life he'd once wanted, the plain family. Was it within his grasp? He shoved the longing down deep. Too many things stood in the way. The bishop didn't understand who he was, how the Englisch world of crime and justice had changed him. How could he ever go back?

He killed the engine and got out. Lucy took Thad inside while Deborah waited for him.

"Dinner is almost ready." Her soft voice sounded unsteady while she kept her attention on the house. He would give anything to know what she was thinking.

"*Gut*, because I am hungry," he said, unable to take his eyes off her.

A hint of a smile touched her pretty mouth, and a delightful color stained her cheeks.

Without answering, she turned on her heel and headed inside. Not exactly the reaction he'd hoped for. He still had work to do to win back her trust. He followed her into the house.

Tantalizing aromas wafted from the kitchen. While Thad set the table, Deborah placed the food onto plates. She'd prepared a chicken pot pie along with the usual accompaniments at an Amish table—fruit preserves, fresh rolls, and other foods she'd likely grown and canned herself.

He leaned past her and picked up two of the plates. Instinctively, she stepped back as if unable to bear his closeness.

Turning away, Eben struggled to come up with something to say to cover the pain of her distance. In the corner of the great room, he noticed a sled. Thad's? He wondered when the boy had gone sledding last.

After the prayer before the meal, he decided to bring it up. "You know, when I was about your age, my best friend and I used to go sledding on the hill close to our community all the time."

In a moment, he had the boy's full attention. "You did? Sledding is my favorite thing to do. My Daed used to take me every year." The boy's face crumpled as he remembered his loss.

"Mine too, though I haven't been in years. We never had a lot of snow in Virginia like you do here, but we made do. I remember one winter my friend Tanner and I decided we'd sneak off and climb up to the top of the big hill where all the older kids went sledding. We believed we could handle it."

He took a bite of still-warm roll while Thad stared at him wide-eyed. "What happened?"

The memory still made him laugh, though at the time he'd been scared to death. "We soon found out we weren't ready for the challenge. Tanner went first. He was always the kind to jump into trouble with both feet. Well, halfway down the hill, Tanner took a tumble. He rolled head over heels until he reached the bottom of the mountain, and I was sure he'd killed himself." He shook his head. "I abandoned my sled and ran as fast as I could to Tanner. By the time I got there, he was half frozen and wailing at the top of his lungs."

"What was wrong with him?" Thad asked.

"Except for a few bumps and bruises, not a thing. But he and I never went near that hill again, even when we were older."

Thad shoved a spoonful of pot pie into his mouth, then chewed it quickly. "Why aren't you Amish anymore?"

"Thad, that's none of our business," Deborah scolded.

"No, it's okay. Thad and I are friends, and he deserves the truth." *So do you.* "My Daed did something wrong, and we were asked to leave our community."

"Did you miss your community when you left?" Thad asked.

"I did. I had to leave my grandparents. That was the hardest part. I loved them so much, and I loved the plain life."

"You can always come back. Maybe you could join our community," Thad said innocently.

Deborah's son was every bit as good, kind, and hopeful as his mother. Words stuck in Eben's throat.

As the silence stretched, Deborah rose and started clearing away the dishes.

"I'm going to step outside and check in with Brian, then take a look around," Lucy told them before excusing herself.

Eben grabbed his and Thad's plates. While Deborah washed, he dried. They worked together without speaking for a while. When the last dish was put away, he didn't know what to say to bridge the wall between them.

She headed to the desk in the great room and returned with a small box. "Thad, how about we work on a puzzle tonight?" She held it up for her son to see.

"Ja! Can Eben help?" Thad asked, emptying the pieces onto the kitchen table.

Eben thought about the surveillance photos waiting on him. As much as he wanted to share this family moment with them, he had work to do. "Maybe next time. You and your Mamm enjoy your puzzle." The disappointment in the boy's eyes made him wish he could have given a different answer.

He went outside and grabbed his sleeping bag and the supplies he'd brought from the house. The night should be interesting. He'd be spending it with a cow, a horse, and a bunch of chickens.

Once he found a spot to spread out the sleeping bag, he brought out surveillance photos taken back when Ed Zachary, aka Henry Yoder, still cooperated with the FBI. He lit a lantern and sat on the sleeping bag to study them.

He'd been over the photos a dozen times, yet Eben couldn't help but believe he'd missed something important in them.

One photo in particular grabbed his attention. Until now, there hadn't been enough information to know what to look for, but now, as he saw this once-insignificant picture for the hundredth time, he gasped. In the photo, Henry Yoder appeared to be wearing the coat that had belonged to Peter. The coat Thad possessed. There was something significant about the coat, yet for the life of him he couldn't understand what. He'd have to examine the coat itself.

With a helpless feeling growing inside, Eben carried the security equipment he'd bought at the store along with his tools inside the house.

The second he came through the door, Thad abandoned his perch at the table and ran over to investigate. "You're back! What's that?" The boy pointed to the bag.

"Something I could use your help with." Eben opened the bag to show him the contents. "We're going to install some extra locks on the front and back door, and then we'll put these latches on the windows."

Thad's eyes lit up. "Can I help Eben, Mamm?"

She sighed gently. "Go ahead. We might as well put the puzzle away for another time."

Eben felt a little guilty for ruining her evening's plans, but he needed them to be as safe as possible. Still, maybe it wouldn't be wise to ask to see her late husband's coat on top of everything. It would have to wait.

The simple task of installing the locks with Thad's help gave Eben a sense of accomplishment. He believed his grandfather would be honored to have instilled in his grandson a sense of pride in working hard. He could almost imagine his grandfather smiling down at him right now.

And he hoped Peter Albrecht was all right with another man teaching his son the same things.

10

"Breakfast, Thad!" Deborah called as she removed biscuits from the oven.

The boy skidded into the kitchen, then frowned. "Where's Eben?"

"I'm sure he'll be here soon," Lucy told him with a chuckle. "It's good to see the two of you getting so close." Lucy winked at Deborah while Thad ambled to the window and peered out.

As excited as Thad was about their upcoming trip to Alamosa to get supplies for the shop, Deborah dreaded the visit, though it would give her a chance to deliver Mrs. Henderson's completed Christmas dress. Normally, it would be just her and Thad on the hours-long buggy ride to the wholesale fabric store, but Eben had insisted on accompanying them today. With her feelings for him changing, being confined to close quarters for so long was not an idea she looked forward to.

Not one she *should* look forward to, anyway.

"There he is!" Thad ran to the door, opening it before Eben could knock. Thad grabbed his hand and practically dragged him to the table. "Come on. Mamm says we have to eat a *gut* breakfast before we leave."

Eben chuckled as he followed Thad. "Looks like someone's excited about our trip." He smiled at Deborah, and she ducked her head. Why did he have to be so handsome?

She'd prepared a simple meal for breakfast—eggs and bacon along with her Mamm's homemade biscuit recipe, and chokecherry preserves.

"I'm going to take another crack at those files while you're gone." Lucy told Eben. "Maybe something will jump out at me that we missed."

Deborah glanced up and caught Eben watching her. Like so many times before, she wished she could read his thoughts.

"Thad, why don't you help me with the dishes?" she asked, to cover her heart's unsteady rhythm.

"No way," Lucy said and rose to her feet. "I can handle the cleanup. You should get on the road before this guy explodes." She tickled Thad, who crumpled into a fit of giggles.

"Are you sure?" Deborah asked. She hated leaving work for Lucy, but mostly she dreaded a long drive at Eben's side when her heart felt this exposed.

"I am sure. Go. Enjoy your day. If anything comes up, I'll give Eben a call."

Accepting Lucy's offer, Deborah gathered her quilted bag and slipped on her cloak. "I will need to stop by the shop to pick up Mrs. Henderson's dress, if you don't mind."

"Fine by me. I'm just happy to be sharing the day with you and Thad." The tenderness in his eyes made her cheeks warm.

Stop it. You can't fall for that again. He's just here to do his job.

"I can't wait to hear about Mrs. Henderson's reaction to the dress. I hope she's pleased," Lucy said and Deborah smiled. Although she'd had to correct some of Lucy's initial stitches, she'd enjoyed helping her friend master the art of sewing.

"She will be surprised to know an Englischer worked on it, especially since your stitches are every bit as neat as mine." Tying her traveling bonnet in place, Deborah handed Thad his coat.

"Ready?" Eben asked.

"Ja, we are ready."

When they stepped outside, the chill of the morning made her shiver despite her warm cloak. Another foot of fresh snow had fallen during the night, covering everything in a white blanket. On days like this, she sometimes felt spring would never come again, and the world would forever be snug and silent.

Thad raced ahead to the car, opening the back door. Once Eben helped Thad buckle his seat belt, he held the door open for her.

Deborah slipped past him, her pulse pounding a crazy beat. What was wrong with her? Eben was there to protect them, nothing more.

Eben walked around to the driver's side and got in. "Will it be like this all winter?"

It would be a long, awkward day if she couldn't find a way to control her foolish heart. She drew in a breath and faced him. "It won't be long, but that is oke, because I love this time of the year. Getting snowed in for days. Making snow ice cream." She winked at her son, whose eyes lit up.

"Ja, snow ice cream is so *gut*."

Eben glanced at the boy in the rearview mirror. "I remember making it with my Mamm too. It was one of my favorite things to do when it snowed. My Mamm would gather the snow, then add condensed milk and vanilla to it. It was wunderbaar," he said with a dreamy smile and Thad giggled at his expression.

"That's how Mamm makes it too, but sometimes we put other things on top, like maple syrup or jam."

As they drove down the isolated road to the community shops, Deborah noticed Eben keeping a careful eye behind them. Unable to stop herself, she glanced over her shoulder.

"There's no one there. I'm just making sure," he whispered so only she could hear. "Relax." He clasped her hand, his warmth engulfing her. "You're safe, I promise."

With him close, she did feel safe. But she also felt other things that weren't safe, not with him.

Eben pulled up in front of her shop and shifted in his seat to face her. "Why don't I go in and get the dress? You and Thad can stay inside where it's warm. Lock the door after me."

While he was trying not to alarm her, she sensed he was on edge, expecting Benson to appear at any time.

Getting out of the car, he waited until she'd pressed down the lock button before heading inside the shop.

"Mamm, I wish Eben could stay with us forever. He makes me not miss Daed so much." Thad's innocent wish made her twist around in her seat. The longing in her son's eyes broke her heart.

"Oh, Thad." Pulling in a breath, she struggled to find the right words to say. "I know you like being with Eben, but he has his own life. A job. A home. Our world is not his anymore. While we appreciate having him here with us now, when the time comes, we must let him go."

Tears welled in Thad's eyes. "But I don't want to let him go."

Deborah leaned back and patted her son's arm. "I know you don't, but we have to do what is best for Eben. We can't be selfish."

Thad scrubbed at his eyes and pulled his arm away, staring out the window, his bottom lip quivering.

She hated seeing her son so upset, especially when she understood how Thad felt. She, too, would be sad when Eben left them. Very, very sad.

Eben came back carrying Mrs. Henderson's completed dress and carefully placed it in the trunk before getting back inside. "It's really getting colder out there." He rubbed his hands together, then blew on them for warmth.

When she didn't answer, he cast a sideways glance at her. "Everything okay?"

She nodded, unable to speak past the lump in her throat conjured by the idea of his impending exit from her life. Eben studied her a moment longer, then put the car in drive and headed out of town.

With Thad uncharacteristically quiet, it felt as if it were just the two of them alone, and the silence became too much.

"Mrs. Henderson lives only a short distance outside of Alamosa. Her husband passed away a few years back. It's just her in that big house alone." The words spewed out in a rush. She expelled a breath and tried to relax. "I called from the community phone to let her know when we would arrive, so she will be expecting us."

Eben nodded, his attention diverted to the road ahead. "The dress is beautiful. I'm sure she will be pleased." He peeked at Thad in the rearview mirror. The boy still gazed out the window. "Hey, Thad, there's a restaurant in Alamosa that serves foot-long sandwiches."

This bit of news grabbed her son's interest right away. "Really?" Thad asked, sitting up. Deborah couldn't help but notice that his eyes were red and swollen from crying.

"Really. I bet you can't finish off a foot of sandwich." Thad immediately perked up at Eben's challenge.

"Can so!"

"We'll see about that." Eben peered over at her. "We might as well enjoy a meal while we're in town, don't you think?"

She didn't know how to answer. The fact that she needed to guard her heart for the days to come when Eben was no longer part of their life made her want to refuse.

"My treat," he told her with an enticing smile.

She managed the tiniest of nods because she really wanted to. "The turnoff for the Circle H Ranch is coming up on your right."

Eben spotted it and entered the elaborate gate leading to Mrs. Henderson's huge two-story log home. He squinted through the windshield. "She must get awfully lonely here alone."

Until last year, Deborah hadn't understood the crippling pain that went along with losing someone you spent much of your life loving.

"I'm sure she does. She has no children of her own. Her niece lives in another state. While he was alive, her husband kept cattle on the property, but she can't manage them by herself, so she doesn't have them anymore. The ranch is slowly dying away."

Eben glanced her way. "That's sad." Something in his tone made her wonder if he were remembering the family he'd lost.

She tilted her head at him, and he cleared his throat.

"Sorry, I was thinking about my grandfather, all alone after my grandmother passed away. I wish I'd been there for him more."

"Eben, you didn't do anything wrong," she whispered.

His mouth twisted. "But I did. I should have stayed behind and taken care of them. If I had, who knows? Maybe both my grandparents would have lived longer. I think losing their entire family all at once just sucked the life out of them."

"You were so young. You did what you thought was best. I'm sure they understood."

"Still, it doesn't change the fact that he died alone."

She could think of nothing to ease his pain. Like her, Eben was a wounded soul carrying his grief close.

He pulled up in front of the house and got out to retrieve the dress from the trunk, with Thad right behind him.

Deborah lifted up a silent prayer for Eben. *Oh Holy Father, his heart is troubled. His pain is well known to You. Console him with Your divine comfort. Amen.*

She got out and joined them at the door.

Mrs. Henderson opened it, expecting them. "Ah, Deborah, there you are. And right on time as always." She enveloped Deborah in a hug, then glanced at Eben and Thad. "And you've brought company."

After introducing Eben to the elderly woman, Deborah said, "And this is my son, Thad."

Eben held out the dress they'd brought.

"Oh, you've outdone yourself!" the older woman exclaimed, her eyes bright. She handed Deborah a cash payment. "I thought the last dress you made for me was lovely, but this one is even more so. I can't wait to wear it to church on Christmas Eve."

"I'm glad you're pleased, Mrs. Henderson. I will have the second dress done in one more week. Thank you for the work."

Clearly sensing the end of the exchange, Thad grabbed Eben's hand and led him back to the gravel driveway.

"It is I who should be thanking you for doing such lovely work," Mrs. Henderson insisted, then glanced past her to where Eben and Thad had crouched to examined some rocks. "He seems like a nice young man. I know how much you miss your husband."

Deborah pivoted, watching her son with Eben. "He is a good man." She ignored Mrs. Henderson's raised brows and thanked her once more for the work, then headed for the car, her heart racing. Mrs. Henderson assumed she and Eben were more than friends, despite the fact that Eben was dressed in Englisch clothes.

"Ready?" Eben straightened and asked.

"Ja, I am ready. Come, Thad, it is time to leave."

The boy pocketed his rocks and climbed back into the car.

Once they were driving again, Deborah tried to push aside her troubled thoughts. Mrs. Henderson, though a sweet lady, had jumped to the wrong conclusion. If she believed there was more to their relationship than friendship after only a few minutes, then what must everyone else in the community be thinking?

"What's the name of the shop?" Eben's deep voice interrupted her thoughts. She glanced up, surprised to find they were on Alamosa's main street.

"Fabric of Life. There." She pointed to the shop ahead on the right.

Eben found a parking spot in front of the shop and slid the car into it.

"You really don't have to go in with me," Deborah insisted, shifting in her seat to look at him. "I made a list of items needed, so I won't be long."

His eyes sparkled as he looked at her. "How about Thad and I hang out here on the sidewalk and watch the people passing by?"

Before she could respond, he exited the car, then opened Thad's door. Her son appeared only too happy to do whatever Eben suggested.

Pulling her door open, Eben held out his hand, his gaze tangling with hers. Warmth spread from their joined hands. As soon as she stepped on the sidewalk, she tugged her hand free and hurried inside.

Samantha Jennings, the shop's owner, came over to greet her. "Deborah, how are you today?"

"I am good," Deborah managed, hoping Samantha didn't notice the red in her cheeks.

"May I help you find something?"

Shaking her head, Deborah took out a piece of paper from her bag. "I have a list. I will look around for a bit."

Samantha smiled and went back behind the counter. "If you need anything, please let me know."

With a nod, Deborah headed to the fabric section first. She needed a special type of fabric for Mrs. Henderson's final dress. Spotting what she wanted, she picked up the bolt of soft, shimmering blue and carried it to the counter.

"Would you cut three yards of this?" she asked Samantha.

"Of course." Samantha took the bolt from her. "This is lovely. Are you making a dress for yourself?"

"No, it's for one of my customers."

"It will make a beautiful one. Your customer is a lucky lady" While

Samantha cut the material, Deborah gathered the rest of the items on her list—fabrics, notions, tools, and other things she thought her customers might enjoy.

"Will that be everything?" Samantha asked as she rang up her purchases.

"Yes, thank you." Deborah took her change. She'd spent a little more than she'd intended, but she knew the items she'd picked up would sell.

"It was good to see you. Come back again." Samantha smiled and Deborah waved goodbye.

Outside, Eben and Thad were counting how many red cars they saw. The sight made her smile.

"Did you get everything you needed?" Eben asked, taking the bags from her.

"Ja, I did. Denki."

He placed the bags inside the car, then relocked the vehicle. "Good, because it's time to see if Thad is up to the challenge."

Thad giggled at Eben's serious expression. "I am."

"Okay." Eben pointed at the restaurant. "It's just across the street." He headed to the intersection, slowing his steps to match hers. His thoughtfulness warmed her heart.

They crossed the street and Eben held the door open for her, his arm brushing hers. A familiar feeling she'd thought dead forever resurfaced, and she ducked her head as she passed by.

The waitress seated them at a table in the corner and handed them each a menu.

Deborah became conscious of several curious glances their way. Even though Alamosa was close to their community, many people still had no idea Amish lived nearby.

"What can I bring you folks today?" the waitress asked.

Deborah picked up the menu, uncertain what to order.

"Do you trust me?" Eben asked.

She nodded and handed him the menu, realizing she did trust him in spite of everything.

"Three meatball subs. Two foot-longs, one regular. And three root beers."

"You got it." The waitress grinned, then took their menus and headed over to the counter.

"Did you get to go to a restaurant like this when you were my age?" Thad asked, his huge round eyes darting around the room in wonder.

"No, never. We had dinner with my grandparents often, but I was seventeen before I ever ate at a restaurant."

Thad's forehead crinkled. "I've been to plenty of restaurants. Did your Daed take you hunting?"

"Yes, he did. Actually, my dad and grandfather both took me hunting. I got my first buck at age seven."

"Whoa. Did your friend Tanner go with you? David's Daed takes him hunting all the time." The wistful look on her son's face was hard to see. She couldn't take him hunting. Maybe she could see if David's family would be willing to take Thad the next time they went.

A small voice inside reminded her that she could try to ignore it all she wanted, but Thad really needed his own Daed.

"Sometimes, but mostly we just played together. We went sledding every chance we could, but after what happened to Tanner that one year, my dad and grandfather usually went with us."

Sadness shadowed Thad's face. "I wish I could go sledding again. Daed always took me. And then we'd build snowmen and have snowball fights."

Deborah remembered how much Peter had enjoyed taking his son sledding.

"If it's okay with your Mamm, I could take you," Eben volunteered. "Perhaps this coming weekend?"

Thad's bright eyes turned to her. "Can he, Mamm?"

The joy on her son's face made it easy to give in. "Are you sure you do not mind?" she asked Eben.

"There is nothing I'd like more. I haven't been sledding in years. It will be nice to be able to act like a child again." His gaze lingered on her face. "You should come as well. It'll be fun, and fun would be good for you."

"Ja, you have to come with us, Mamm." Thad begged.

"We'll see," she said without looking at Eben.

Their meals arrived and Thad's mouth formed a perfect *O* as he surveyed the foot-long sandwich and french fries.

"Prayers first," Deborah chided, hiding her amusement when Thad snuck a French fry. He folded his hands in his lap and chewed, obviously trying to hide that he was doing so.

For the first time, Deborah didn't know what to pray. She wanted things that were not hers to ask for, and she was in desperate need of Gött's strength.

Heavenly Father, please make me strong in my weakness.

Eben echoed her *Amen* and their eyes met. She would live in the present and not look to the future and the pain that waited for both her and her son there.

Thad gripped the sandwich with both small hands and took a huge bite, sauce dripping down his chin. Deborah covered her smile.

"What do you think?" Eben asked, chuckling at the boy's expression.

"It's wunderbaar," he said with his mouth full.

Eben shifted his intense gaze her way. "And you? Are you enjoying your meal?"

She wiped her hands on her napkin. "Ja, it is *gut*, but there is no way I can finish this sandwich, much less a foot-long." She shook her head and he chuckled.

"I'm afraid I may not be up to the task myself either." He peered at Thad, who had almost finished his. "Slow down. I'm declaring you the winner already."

Thad giggled and finished off the last of his meal. "That was easy."

"Oh, yeah?" Eben pushed his plate away. "Well, not for me." He patted his stomach. "No more room."

When the waitress brought their bill, Deborah brought out her wallet, but Eben refused her offer to pay. "Put your money away. This is my treat."

"Denki," she murmured, then nudged Thad to do the same.

As they prepared to leave, a man entered the restaurant and looked around, as if searching for someone in particular. His eyes lit on them, and he made his way toward their table.

"Eben." Deborah nodded toward the man.

"Brian." Eben rose to his feet, clearly surprised by the man's appearance but covering it quickly. "Deborah, Thad, this is Brian Anderson, my commander."

The man extended his hand to Deborah. "It's nice to meet you both. Can I have a minute?" he asked Eben.

"Of course. I'll be right back," Eben told them, and the two men left the restaurant.

The man's sudden appearance served as another reminder of why Eben was there. He didn't belong among the Amish any longer. In time, he would be gone. And she would be left to pick up the pieces for both herself and her son.

"What's up?" Eben asked once they were out of earshot. It had to be bad for Brian to track him down.

Brian motioned toward the woman and child who had occupied so much of Eben's thoughts lately. "How are they holding up?"

Eben followed his line of sight. Both Deborah and Thad watched their exchange. He couldn't imagine the thoughts going through Deborah's head.

"They're okay. I think getting away for the day helped. The incident at the barn really spooked Deborah."

"I can imagine. That's one of the reasons why I'm here. In light of what happened, I spoke with Bishop Timothy again and got his approval to call in extra agents. They've been searching the surrounding countryside for Benson."

"Have they found anything yet?" Eben asked, hoping for answers.

Brian gave a terse shake of his head. "Benson seems to have disappeared into thin air, along with Henry Yoder."

Not for a minute did Eben believe Benson had fled the area. "He's still around. He needs something, and there's too much at stake for him to leave without it." He told Brian about the photo showing Henry wearing the same coat that now belonged to Thad. "I'm sure there's a connection, but I haven't had the chance to examine the coat in private yet, and without Henry Yoder's input, we might never know its importance." Eben shook his head. "The last person to see Yoder was Thad on the day Benson attacked him. If Benson has him, his days are numbered." He didn't add *if they aren't already over*, but his commander's expression said he was thinking it anyway.

Brian glanced at the passing foot traffic. "That's what I wanted to talk to you about. I need you to head up the hunt for Yoder."

After what had happened at the farm, Eben didn't want to leave Deborah and Thad to someone else's care. "I won't leave them unprotected." He glanced Deborah's way. Uncertainty covered her face as she watched him and Brian. He'd give anything to be able to reassure her everything would work out.

"They won't be. We'll have agents watching them at all times. Plus, Lucy is there. I don't think Benson will dare show his face anywhere near the house again."

Eben wasn't nearly as confident in other agents' commitment to protecting the Albrechts as he was in his own. "I plan to sleep in the barn still. If that isn't satisfactory, then I can't do the job."

Brian didn't reply for a moment, studying Eben's face. Finally, he gave in, "Whatever you want. You're the best agent I have. I need you on this yesterday. We have to find Yoder and fast, before Benson kills him. Without him we have nothing."

11

Eben was unusually quiet the entire trip home, barely speaking more than a handful of words. Something had happened during that conversation with his commander. Deborah prayed it wasn't bad news.

Thad chattered on, seemingly oblivious to the change in Eben, excited about their upcoming sledding trip.

When she could bear Eben's silence no longer, she murmured, "Is everything oke?"

He shook his head without looking at her. Was it part of the job to keep parts of yourself hidden from those closest to you?

Deborah's thoughts traveled back over the day. It had been a happy one, in spite of some residual hurt feelings and the appearance of Eben's commander. She stole a glance Eben's way. A frown creased his handsome forehead, and his jaw was locked tight. Her heart clenched at the trouble in his eyes.

Near the house, a dark sedan was parked at the edge of the road near her drive. She gripped the armrest. Had Benson come back?

"It's okay. It's one of ours," Eben told her, quietly so as not to alarm Thad. As they passed the car, she noticed two men inside.

Eben turned onto her drive and slowed his speed. More snow had fallen while they were gone, piling up along the road. The car slipped and slid along the way.

They'd barely come to stop when Thad hopped out. Clutching her purchases against her chest, Deborah forced the door open against a bracing wind.

Thad tugged at Eben's sleeve. "Come see the sled my Daed built for me."

"Not right now. I need to speak with your Mamm alone first."

Thad's face fell at Eben's stern tone. He turned away, shoulders slumped.

Blowing out a sigh, Eben knelt in front of the boy. "I'm sorry. I would love to see your sled, but first I must speak with your Mamm. I'll be right in, okay?"

The boy beamed again. *He's too attached to Eben.*

"Oke." Thad ran up the steps and disappeared inside.

When the door closed, Eben faced her, the look in his eyes frightening.

"Something's happened," she said. It wasn't a question. "That's why your commander wanted to speak with you."

"Yes. He's added more men to watch the house," he said, then hesitated. "And Brian wants me to head up the search for Henry Yoder."

She stared at him, trying to understand what this meant. "You're leaving?" The words were impossible to get out.

He took her hands. "No, I'll be here every evening. I'm just focusing on a different area of the case."

She swallowed and stared at their joined hands. Perhaps not now, but one day, he would leave for good. This felt like the beginning of that.

"And I still plan to take Thad sledding this weekend. I would never disappoint the boy. He's too important to me. I hope you will come as well." His voice softened as he said the words, sending her heart soaring. "In the meantime, while I'm away during the day, Lucy will be with you at the shop, and another agent will be stationed outside the school. There will be extra agents covering the house as well. You'll be safe, I promise."

"But you won't be here to make sure." The words tumbled out before she could stop them.

"Not all the time, but Lucy is one of the best agents I know, and she'll have plenty of backup."

Deborah wished she shared his outlook. "I should go inside. I need to start dinner."

When she would have pulled away, Eben clasped her hands tight. She glanced up. There was something more. "What is it?"

His mouth twisted, as if he were trying to figure out how to say what he needed to. "Did Peter ever mention knowing Henry Yoder or Ed Zachary before?"

The question surprised her. "No, never. Why?"

Eben removed a photo from his pocket and showed it to her. It showed Henry dressed as an Englischer. What he wore threatened to buckle her knees. Henry had on the same coat he'd recently given to Thad. The coat that had belonged to Peter.

Until Thad told her what Henry said about working with his father, Deborah had no idea that Peter even knew Henry. "I don't understand. Why is Henry wearing Peter's coat? I thought he told Thad he'd found it and planned to return it after the accident, but that's clearly not the case." She shook her head. "What's going on?"

Eben blew out a breath. "I wish I knew. Perhaps nothing, but this is strange, to say the least. We need to find Henry and determine the connection between the coat and Benson. Thad said Henry pushed both the coat and him out of sight when he saw Benson. That tells me he wanted to keep the coat out of Benson's hands. There's something important about it, but I'm not sure Benson knows that that's what he's looking for." He paused for a breath, then said, "I need to take a look at it now."

Deborah didn't hesitate. "Of course. I'll get it for you." A shiver raced down her spine as she and Eben went inside.

"There you two are." Lucy was in the foyer, slipping into her jacket. "Thad's in his room. I'm going to check around the perimeter and have a word with the other agents. I'll be back soon," she told them and hurried outside.

Deborah went to Thad's room and found him reading on his bed. "Thad, may I borrow your coat? I'll bring it back when I'm done."

The boy smiled at her. "Oke, Mamm."

She grabbed the coat from the hook on the wall where Thad had neatly hung it up and handed it to Eben. He looked the coat over carefully before shaking his head. "There's nothing here. I don't get it."

Deborah took the coat and hung it by the door as regret settled into the pit of her stomach. She'd had no idea that her husband's life had been taken in such a brutal way. She thought about the days before Peter's death. He'd been withdrawn and preoccupied. At the time, she'd assumed it was because of his work. On the day of the accident, Peter hadn't wanted to take Thad with him, but the boy had been so disappointed that he'd changed his mind. Did Peter suspect what Benson had planned?

It broke her heart to think of her son carrying such a horrible burden for the past year. As much as she wanted to speak with Thad about what he'd witnessed, the thought of her boy having to relive the final moments before his Daed's death was too much.

No matter what, she wouldn't make her son go through that. She'd fight Eben and the entire FBI if necessary, but she wouldn't put Thad through that again.

The meal was a quiet one. Eben barely touched his food. The following day had him worried. He wouldn't be there for Deborah and Thad. What if something happened while he was away?

"Would you like some coffee?" Deborah's soft voice interrupted his troubled thoughts.

He shook his head. "It's getting late and I should be going. I'll take a quick look around outside, then turn in."

Disappointment marred her lovely face. He believed she'd enjoyed their day together as well.

"But you promised to look at my sled," Thad said, the same disappointment from earlier written on his face.

"You're right. I would love to see your sled," Eben assured him with a smile.

Thad scraped back his chair. "I'll get it." He hurried to the mudroom off the back door.

A hint of a smile touched Deborah's face. "He's so proud of the sled. He and his Daed worked on it for weeks." The pain he saw in her was hard to take. Jealousy roared to life as emotions he had no right to feel made him wonder if she would ever be free to love gain.

He struggled for something to say. "I'm sorry about your husband, Deborah. I can't even imagine."

She averted her gaze. "Not a day goes by when I don't miss him." She seemed about to say something more, but Thad ran back into the room carrying a well-worn sled. He held it up for Eben to see, smiling proudly.

Eben lifted the sled from the boy's arms and admired it. "Wow, now this is a nice one. I bet it goes really fast."

Thad eagerly nodded. "Ja, it's a beauty!"

Eben examined it carefully, noticing one of the skids appeared loose. "If you want, I can tighten this skid for you before Saturday. It won't take long. I would hate for that to come off. You might get hurt."

Thad stared up at him for the longest time before nodding. "Ja, I wouldn't want to be like Tanner and go tumbling down the hill."

Eben chuckled at the boy's memory. "That wouldn't be good. Why don't I take the sled with me and I'll fix it for you?"

With Thad's approval, Eben tucked it under his arm. "Now, I'd better get out of here so that you and your Mamm can get some sleep. Tomorrow is a school day."

"Aw, do you have to go?" Thad's shoulders sank.

"I'm afraid I do. A good night's rest will help you do well in school."

Thad ran to Eben and threw his arms around his waist. "I can't wait to tell David about our sledding trip." Stunned by Thad's affection, Eben watched the boy hurry away with a lump in his throat. It amazed him, the depth of love he felt for a young boy who had lost so much.

"I'd better go," he told Deborah, his voice unsteady.

Deborah walked him to the door. "It was a nice day," she said with regret. It made him happy that she didn't want the day to end either.

He realized with a jolt that he'd give anything to be able to call her his Fraa. Share her life. Be there for her and Thad from that day forward. "It's a day I won't ever forget. Thank you for letting me go with you and Thad."

The soulful look in her eyes deepened the longings of his heart. Before he could stop himself, he gently touched her cheek, holding her gaze a moment longer, memorizing every detail of her lovely face. Then, he turned and walked out before he did something really stupid, like listen to his heart's clamors to kiss her. The door closed behind him. His chest tightened.

Flicking on the flashlight, Eben surveyed the area around the front of the house. Nothing appeared out of place. As he headed for the barn, he noticed Lucy coming from the woods nearby. At first she didn't notice him until he flashed the light her way. She stopped dead in her tracks, then came over to him.

"No sign of Benson?" he asked.

"Oh, no. Nothing. All is quiet," she said without hesitation.

Something about her demeanor seemed off, but Eben dismissed it. He sometimes wondered if Lucy wasn't bucking for his job, taking on more than she was ready for. The old him would have challenged her motives. But since this case—well, the things that mattered to him were changing. The job no longer held the appeal it once did.

"Are you ready for tomorrow?" Lucy asked.

"I believe so." He updated her on what Brian had asked him to do. "We'll be checking on some of Benson's lesser-known hangouts to start with. Do you have things covered on this end? She'll be vulnerable at the shop, like Thad will be at school."

"I've got it, Eben. Trust me, I know what I'm doing. Benson's not going to harm her or Thad on my watch."

He inclined his head while trying to ignore the doubts crowding in. "Good. I'll see you in the morning. We'll go over things before I leave." Whether Lucy liked it or not, he wouldn't go until they'd covered every possible scenario and how she'd handle it.

"Eben, I can protect Deborah and Thad. You just find Yoder."

He bid her good night and went to the barn, where darkness and familiar scents greeted him. Somehow, Deborah's barn already felt more like home than the house he'd been restoring with his own two hands.

He picked up the lantern he'd left by the door and lit it. "Hello, Cinnamon," Eben said to the cow, who watched him with mild interest. The chickens had found their roost for the night. Bridget, the family's mare, whinnied from her stall.

Placing the sled next to the door, Eben carried a bucket of oats over to Bridget and the mare Lucy had borrowed, stroking Bridget's muzzle while she ate. "Looks like it's just us, girls."

Tossing the cow some hay, Eben settled down with the files once more. The feeling that the answers they needed were right under his nose wouldn't go away, yet after more than an hour, nothing new jumped out at him. What was he missing with the coat?

He put the files away and unzipped his sleeping bag. Tomorrow promised to be a long, grueling day, made worse by not being able to keep an eye on the Albrechts himself. Blowing out the lantern, he settled into the sleeping bag, but the stillness around him had him on edge.

When he closed his eyes, Deborah's lovely face appeared before him. He'd enjoyed the day immensely. If it weren't for the danger crowding in, they might have appeared to be any normal family on an outing. The word stuck in his thoughts. Normal. For ten years he'd told himself his life as an FBI agent fulfilled him. While his career flourished, he'd shoved his plain roots aside and pretended this life he lived was normal, yet he hadn't been truly happy in a long time. The evil he dealt with on a daily basis went against every part of his upbringing.

Rolling to his side, Eben listened to the noises of the night—an occasional cluck from the chicken coop, the howl of a wolf in the distance. The warmth of the sleeping bag was a stark contrast to the cold night. With his mind unable to shut off, he reviewed the details of the case.

Why had Benson killed Peter? The only explanation was that Peter must have known something about Benson's crimes. But what?

His thoughts shifted to Henry Yoder. At the time of his disappearance as Ed Zachary, the FBI believed Benson had gotten wind of Yoder's betrayal and killed him. Instead, Yoder had gone into hiding, changing his name and taking up residence among the Amish—a drastic move, but the last place Benson would think to search for him.

Eben prayed Henry was still alive. Without his assistance, they might never know the reason behind Peter's death without forcing

Thad to talk, and Eben couldn't put the boy through reliving that dreadful day. In time, when Thad wished to talk about it, perhaps, but not before.

Giving up on sleep for the time being, Eben decided to take another look around outside. Nothing stirred, yet the niggling of unease in the pit of his stomach wouldn't let him rest.

Up at the house, a faint light shone through the curtains. Someone else couldn't sleep either. Eben hurried up the steps and knocked quietly, trying not to wake anyone else.

To his surprise, Thad opened the door. "Hi, Eben!"

"What are you doing up?" Eben asked, following the boy to the great room. He appeared to be reading by the light of the woodstove.

"I couldn't sleep, but I didn't want to wake up Mamm or Lucy."

"Is something bothering you?" Eben sat in the rocker next to Thad.

The boy didn't look at him. "Mamm told me you are working on something else for a while. She said I might not see you as much." Tears filled Thad's eyes. "But I don't want you to leave." The sight of Thad's bottom lip quivering ripped Eben's heart to shreds.

Eben knelt in front of the boy and gathered him close. "I'll still see you. I'm not leaving the community. I'm just going to be working on a different part of the investigation. But I'll be here every evening. We'll still see each other at dinner."

Thad peered up at him. "You mean it?"

Eben struggled to get words out. "I sure do. In fact, why don't I go get your sled right now, and we'll work on it together since we're both up. We just have to be careful not to wake your Mamm or Lucy, okay?"

Thad eagerly nodded.

"Good. I'll be right back. Come lock the door behind me."

"Can I come with you?"

Eben weighed the wisdom of Thad's request. He could be putting

Thad's life in danger, but one look at the boy's wishful expression and he didn't have the heart to say no. "Okay, but stay close, and we have to hurry. I don't want your Mamm to wake up and find you gone. She'd worry. Put on your coat."

Thad eagerly shoved his arms into his coat, and they stepped outside. Fresh snow drifted down through the darkness. Thad stuck out his tongue to catch the snowflakes. Eben smiled at the boy's innocent gesture.

A twig snapped close by, immediately putting Eben on alert. "Stay close to me," he told Thad. Eben shined the light around where he'd heard the noise.

A buck stared back at them briefly, then ran away.

"It's just a deer," Thad said.

Eben's training robbed him of the relief he should have felt. "Perhaps." He grabbed the sled and the tools he'd need to repair it, then on impulse, picked up his sleeping bag.

"Why are you bringing your sleeping bag?" Thad asked, trotting to keep up with his brisk strides on the way back to the house.

"Because I'd like to bunk down in front of the fire tonight to stay warm."

The boy didn't question his answer.

Once they were safe inside, he peered out the window. Nothing but darkness. So why couldn't he relax?

Eben carried the sled to the table and turned it upside down so he could work.

"Can I see your gun?" Thad asked, the question taking Eben by surprise.

Hesitating, he removed it from his pocket and showed it to Thad.

The boy's eyes grew large. "Can I hold it? I know how to hold a gun. My Daed showed me."

"Not this one, and you should never play with guns, Thad. They are not toys."

Thad nodded solemnly. "Oke, Eben."

Placing the gun back inside his pocket, Eben had an idea. "Thad, do you know what to do if someone tries to grab you?"

The boy stared up at him with huge eyes, shaking his head.

"Okay, then I'm going to show you." He clutched Thad tight, restricting his arms. "Do you know how to break free?"

Thad struggled against his hold, but couldn't budge.

"This is what you do. You have two feet free. If someone has you in a hold like this, you stomp on their foot with all your might, or kick them hard in the shin. Once they let you go, run as fast as you can and don't stop for anything. Do you understand?"

"But Mamm says hurting people is wrong," Thad protested.

The Amish upbringing—to them, violence was wrong. But not when it could save this boy from meeting the same fate his father had. "She's right. But it's okay if a bad man tries to pick you up and you don't want to go with him. It won't hurt him much. You're just trying to startle him into letting go. Would it make you feel better if your Mamm and I talked about it?"

"Ja."

"Then we'll do that. In the meantime, let's give it a try." Still clutching the boy tight, Eben asked, "What do you do?"

Thad didn't hesitate. "I stomp on their foot or kick their leg, and then I run."

"That's right." Eben let him go. "Good boy. Remember that." He prayed Thad would never have to put his training to the test. "Now, let's see if we can fix that sled before Saturday."

By the time they'd finished the repairs, the boy's eyes had begun to droop.

"Off to bed you go. Tomorrow is a school day, and we have chores to do before you and your Mamm leave."

"Oke." Thad took only a few steps before he came back to Eben and threw his arms around his waist. "I'm glad you're not leaving," Thad murmured, then spun and ran to his room. The simple show of affection made the thought of leaving the boy once the assignment was over unbearable.

Being back among the plain people made Eben's desire to return even stronger. Was it possible? In his heart he knew he wanted to try, whether he had a future with Deborah and Thad or not. Either way, he knew he wanted to be Amish again.

But he also knew that he wanted the Albrechts to be his family. He just prayed he could convince Deborah that his feelings had nothing to do with playing a part for the job.

12

Nothing would have prepared Deborah for finding Eben asleep in her great room. She stopped and watched him for a moment, entranced by his handsome face relaxed in sleep. He appeared at peace, reminding her of the way things had been between them the day before. At least until his commander showed up. She'd enjoyed their day together a little too much. Going over every look, every word had kept her awake long into the night.

Eben mumbled something in his sleep, then stirred. She hurried to the kitchen, not wanting him to catch her watching him.

Grabbing a skillet, she brought the apples from the refrigerator that she'd sliced the night before to make her son's favorite, apple ring fritters, for breakfast.

She was dipping the apple rings into the batter when Eben appeared in the kitchen's entrance. Their eyes met. Something unreadable flared in his gaze. When heat crawled into her cheeks, she focused on the task of battering the apples.

"I'm sorry," he said, his voice husky with sleep. "I planned to be gone before you woke, but I guess I was more tired than I thought."

To this she had no answer. She couldn't say it was all right because it was inappropriate to have him sleeping in the house when she didn't have a husband. But she couldn't protest either, since she knew he'd only done it to protect her.

She avoided having to answer by placing the battered apple slices in the pan to fry.

"I took a look around the place last night when I noticed a light on inside the house. I came to check it out and found Thad awake," he continued.

She whirled to face him. "What?"

"He just couldn't sleep. We worked on the sled together until we were both tired, and I fell asleep here."

She sensed he wasn't telling her everything. "Did something else happen last night?"

He stepped closer, and Deborah struggled to keep from moving away.

"I thought I heard something outside last night," he said in a low voice.

Everything else forgotten, she asked, "Was it Benson?"

"No, only a deer. Still, I thought it best to stay close."

She searched his eyes. What wasn't he saying?

Before she could form the question, Thad bounded into the room. "I'm ready to do our chores," he sang out.

Was it her imagination, or did Eben seem relieved by Thad's appearance? "Then let's get started. Your Mamm will have breakfast ready soon enough."

Thad's eyes lit up. "Apple ring fritters! Denki, Mamm." He hugged her with enthusiasm, then he and Eben headed for the door together.

"Wait." Both turned. "Eben, are you sure?" She couldn't be more specific than that without alarming her son.

"He'll be fine. I'm with him and I won't let anything happen."

The tenderness in his eyes stole her breath away. She managed a tiny nod, then turned away.

Once she finished frying the apples, she sprinkled cinnamon and sugar over them. Grabbing some eggs from the refrigerator, she cracked them into a bowl just as Lucy came in.

"I'm sorry I overslept. I wanted to help you with breakfast."

Deborah smiled sympathetically. "It's okay. You can scramble these while I put on the Kaffe."

Lucy nodded, then took the bowl from her. "I'm going to miss your coffee when this assignment ends."

"As much as I want you to capture this man, I will regret us having to say goodbye."

Lucy stopped what she was doing and gave Deborah a hug. "I know. I'm going to miss you as well. Perhaps I can stop by from time to time and we can catch up. Have some Kaffe together."

Deborah grinned at the awkward way Lucy said the word. "I would like that." She'd had no idea when she'd welcomed Lucy into her life that she would become so attached to the younger woman.

"Where is Thad?" Lucy asked.

"He and Eben are doing the morning chores." Deborah finished preparing the coffee and took the silverware from the drawer.

"They sure have taken to each other. Thad will miss having him around. And I'm guessing you will as well." Lucy's knowing gaze found hers, and Deborah struggled to keep her attention on setting the table.

"Eben's a *gut* man, but he has his life. And we have ours."

"Uh-huh," Lucy said, but didn't press the matter. "Do you think you'll ever marry again?"

The question surprised Deborah. Until Eben had come into their lives, the thought of sharing her life with another man felt impossible. She'd believed bringing Thad up the way Peter would have wanted was Gött's plan for her life now. But Eben made her wish things could be different.

"I know you miss your husband," Lucy said softly, "but you're still young, and you could have other children. You have such a good heart, and it seems wasteful for you not to share it with a good man.

There might be one who could give you the love you need, even if it doesn't make sense to anyone else."

Before she could reply, voices wafted their way, both Thad's high one and Eben's deep one. Her son really loved the man who had come into their lives so unexpectedly, and she believed Eben felt the same way about Thad.

Wiping her hands on her apron, she straightened her prayer Kapp as the door opened. Cold air rushed in ahead of them. The sight of Eben standing beside her son, so handsome and strong, filled her with longing. She averted her eyes, pretending to check the coffee.

"Mamm, look at all the eggs we gathered." Thad carefully carried a basket over for her to admire.

"Oh, now that is a lot." She grinned at her son, aware of Eben standing close with a pail of fresh milk.

"All the chores are done, thanks to Thad." Eben poured the milk into a pitcher, then washed out the pail.

"Go wash up, Thad," Deborah said, hoping her voice sounded normal when Eben's nearness and how he fit into their morning routine had brought her heart into her throat.

"I'll go with you." Eben followed the boy from the room.

While she placed food on plates, Lucy poured coffee for the adults and milk for Thad.

Eben returned. "Here, I'll take those to the table." He took two of the plates from her, his hand brushing hers. The now-familiar awareness sparked between them as their eyes held, and for a moment she forgot to breathe.

Thad rushed into the room. "Eben and I are going to clean out the barn when he gets home tonight." The boy beamed. Deborah couldn't remember the last time she'd seen him so happy.

"That's wunderbaar," Deborah told him. "Denki." *For everything. For making my son happy, for making sure we're safe, for all of it.*

As they ate, Thad filled them in on how he and Eben had fixed his sled.

"I'm sure you were a big help," Deborah said, barely hearing the words, her thoughts a million miles away.

When they had finished, Eben grabbed her plate and his and carried them to the sink to wash.

"You don't have to do that," she said, as had become her habit.

"I know, but I want to." He washed the first dish while Deborah took the towel from its holding place to dry. When the cleanup was finished, Eben shouldered into his coat and headed for the door. "I should go. Thad, be good for your Mamm today. Lucy, can I have a word with you outside?"

Lucy nodded and followed him out the door.

"I wish I could go with Eben," Thad said when it was just the two of them.

Deborah knelt in front of him. "I know you like being with Eben, but he has a job to do." She hesitated, hating that she had to remind Thad of the truth. "You know, someday Eben will leave our community. As much as we like having him here, we can't keep him from his life."

"But I don't want him to leave." Tears filled the boy's eyes, and she drew him close.

"I know you don't, but that is not our decision to make."

"I'm going to pray for Gött to make him stay."

"Thad, we pray for Gött to give us what we need and what's best for us, not just what we want."

"Eben staying *is* what's best for us." He pulled free and ran to his room.

Frustrated, Deborah rose to her feet. Perhaps Thad needed to spend more time with his Grossdaddi. She would speak to him about it.

Lucy came back inside with another man Deborah didn't recognize.

"Deborah, this is Agent Stephens. He'll be accompanying us to town. He'll keep an eye on Thad today. We've cleared it with Bishop Timothy, who let Thad's teacher know as well."

"It's nice to meet you, ma'am. If you're ready, we should be on our way."

Deborah turned. With everything happening she couldn't imagine going about her daily routine as if everything was oke. "I'll just go get Thad."

She knocked on her son's door and opened it. "Thad, time to go."

Without a word, the boy hopped off the bed and followed her to the great room, the evidence of tears plain on his face. Deborah introduced him to Agent Stephens, who kept his response short and professional. If Thad's expression was anything to go by, he was comparing the impersonal Agent Stephens to the irreplaceable Eben.

Just like she was.

On the trip in to town today, Lucy and Agent Stephens talked little, and all of Deborah's attempts at drawing Thad out of his misery proved useless.

Agent Stephens stopped the car in front of the shop. "I'll drop you two off, and then Thad and I will drive to the school together. I will stay in the car outside the schoolhouse so I don't disrupt the lessons. You know how to reach me if you need anything," he added to Lucy. She nodded and got out.

Deborah leaned over and kissed Thad's cheek. "I will see you in a little while. Do what Agent Stephens tells you to do, oke?" When the boy didn't answer, she sighed and climbed out of the car. Agent Stephens drove off.

Deborah unlocked the shop door and went inside, putting her things away.

"Are you okay?" Lucy asked, a frown line appearing between her brows. Deborah knew she was being unusually quiet, but her heart broke for her son.

"Ja, just worried about Thad."

"He'll be okay. Agent Stephens is one of our best." Lucy placed a hand on her arm, then headed to the workroom to make sure it was safe. "Everything's clear back there. I might as well make myself useful and straighten up the bolts of material."

"Denki," Deborah murmured, then carried the fabric she'd purchased for Mrs. Henderson's other dress to the cutting table. The pattern, though simple, was one of her favorites. She carefully laid out the material and pinned the pattern to it. As she cut, her thoughts drifted to Eben. She missed knowing he was close and wondered what he was doing right now.

Was he in danger?

The thought made her cut where she hadn't meant to. It was fixable, but she needed to keep her mind on her work.

Once she finished cutting out the last piece of the pattern, she noticed Lucy slipping out the front door without a word. Confused, Deborah hurried to the window and saw Lucy heading away from the shops.

After putting a *Be Right Back* sign in the window, Deborah locked up the shop, fearing Lucy might be in trouble. As she approached where she'd last seen her friend, Deborah heard her voice and stopped to listen.

"We're still searching for Henry Yoder."

Deborah just caught the words. Lucy must be discussing the case with one of her fellow agents. Relieved, Deborah went back to the shop.

When Lucy returned a little while later, she appeared distracted. "Is everything okay?" Deborah asked.

Lucy's smile seemed forced. "Of course. I just needed to check on something. Everything's under control. Don't worry." She glanced at the cut fabric. "You're ready to start sewing."

"Ja, I am. I thought we'd have lunch first, then you can help me if you'd like."

"Oh fun. I'll be able to make my own clothes by the time I leave here."

Deborah bit her bottom lip to keep from chuckling. Lucy was still a long way from making her own clothing. She grabbed the picnic basket of fried chicken, green beans, and macaroni and cheese she'd prepared for their lunch.

Though there was no way to know whether Lucy actually joined in the silent prayer, the younger woman bowed her head out of respect. When Deborah uttered "Amen," Lucy picked up a piece of chicken and bit into it. "This is so good. I'm getting quite plump with all the delicious food. Before I came here, I don't remember the last time I enjoyed a home-cooked meal. We keep strange hours at the Bureau." She sighed wistfully. "In many ways, I wish I could live like you. It's so simple and peaceful here. I'd love to run away and live this type of life forever."

The expression on Lucy's face made Deborah reach for her hand and squeeze it. "I can't imagine living any other way."

Lucy lifted her shoulders. "I guess we're both exactly where we're supposed to be."

Once they'd cleared away the meal, Lucy said, "I'll come help with the dress after I finish organizing the fabric. I'm almost done, and I actually really enjoyed it."

Deborah went back to work on Mrs. Henderson's dress, and the time passed quickly. Yet, for some reason, every little noise had her jumping and checking the windows. She couldn't shake the feeling that something bad was about to happen.

Eben's safety was foremost in her mind. If something happened to him while he looked out for them, she didn't think she could bear it.

Deborah strode to the work room to get the thread she needed for the dress. In passing, she glanced out the window. What she saw there froze her in place. Something moved. As she peered into the shadows, she noticed a man staring at the shop.

At her.

Without a doubt, she knew it was Benson.

"Lucy!" Deborah screamed.

Lucy ran to her side. "What is it?"

She pointed to the woods. "There's someone out there."

"Get out of sight and lock the door behind me." Lucy drew her weapon and slipped out the door.

Deborah quickly relocked it and leaned against it, her heart pounding in her chest.

It felt as if hours passed with no word. Where was Lucy? Was she safe?

The knock on the back door startled her. She stifled a scream.

"It's me, Deborah. It's okay to open the door."

Deborah fumbled with the lock, then pulled the door open.

"Was it him?" she asked as Lucy closed the door.

"No, one of our agents, actually. Benson's not out there. You're safe."

But the uneasy feeling inside wouldn't allow her that peace of mind. Would there ever be a time when she felt safe again?

When the Amish community came into view, he let out a weary sigh. The day had been grueling as Eben and his four-member team searched each of Benson's holdings, but found no evidence Benson or anyone else had been there in a while. To make matters worse, the weather had hindered their search efforts most of the day. With more snow on the way, Eben and some of his men were looking deeper into the connection between Peter and Yoder, reviewing all the video surveillance they could find to see if there was any conversation between the two men. But there were few cameras in small, mostly-Amish towns, so they hadn't found anything yet.

Frustrated at the day's lack of results, Eben stifled a yawn. All he wanted was to see Deborah's smiling face, chat with Thad, and enjoy the things that mattered to him. He couldn't wait until Saturday to take the boy sledding.

He'd spoken to Lucy earlier. Their day had been uneventful. Both Deborah and Thad were safe at home. Still, until he could see for himself, he wouldn't be able to relax.

But first, he needed to do something.

Parking in front of the diner, he climbed out. As much as he wanted to continue the work he'd started at the diner, with this new project, he didn't feel he could do both.

Pulling in a deep breath, Eben opened the door and went inside. Samuel and Gertie were eating at one of the tables.

When Samuel spotted him, he stood and clapped Eben on the back. "It is *gut* to see you, my friend. I did not expect a visit today."

"I know," he murmured, dreading what must be done. He considered Samuel and Gertie his friends.

"Is something wrong?" Samuel asked, correctly reading Eben's expression. He pointed to the table. "Sit. Please. Would you like something to eat?"

Eben shook his head. "No thank you. I can't stay. I just wanted to stop by and tell you in person that I don't think I can continue to work for you." He shared what he could about the search with the couple.

"I am sorry to hear that, but I understand. You have a job that must come first. This man has to be brought to justice," Samuel said.

Eben inclined his head. "Thank you for being so understanding. I'll miss working with you and Gertie each day."

Samuel's grin took the concern away. "And we will miss you as well, but you are doing *gut* work. Important work that you were meant to do."

Eben had once believed the same thing.

"But it is not what you want to do anymore, is it?" Samuel said softly, his sharp eyes clearly seeing what Eben could no longer hide.

"No it isn't," he said quietly. He'd told the couple about his wish to return to his Amish roots and his discussion with the bishop. "But I'm afraid I've messed things up. Perhaps it's too late for me."

Samuel shook his head. "Nay, it is not too late. If you truly desire to return to this way of life, you can. Gött specializes in second chances. Speak with Bishop Timothy and let him guide you."

Eben rose to his feet. "Thanks. You and Gertie are good friends, and I'm sorry to leave before the job is finished."

Samuel waved his hands in dismissal. "Do not worry about the job. It will be finished in Gött's time."

With a smile, Eben waved to his friend, then headed back to his car, where his mind circled back to the case.

He had never felt so helpless before. At every turn, they were met with another dead end. The pressure to capture Benson before he came after Deborah and Thad again built within him until he thought he would burst. He was in desperate need of something to work through his frustration before facing Deborah again.

He drove to the Glick house, climbed out, and went inside. After lighting the lantern by the door, Eben glanced around the place. The work he'd done so far made him proud. The place was actually livable again. With most of the repairs finished, there was just one more thing left to do.

Bringing his tools in from the car, Eben went to work on the sagging door in the bedroom and let the simple task of working with his hands soothe away the troubles from his soul.

13

"Where is Eben?" Thad asked for the second time in minutes. "He promised to help me clean up the barn."

"I don't know. Perhaps something came up," Deborah said, her heart breaking for her boy. It was so unlike Eben not to follow through on his word. She cleared away the last of the meal, saving Eben a plate.

"I spoke to him earlier. I'm sure he'll be here soon," Lucy said.

Headlights flashed across the front of the house, and Thad ran to the window.

"It's him!" Before Deborah could stop him, Thad bounded outside.

Deborah followed in time to see her son leap into Eben's arms. "Thad!" she called.

"He's all right," Eben said with a chuckle. "I don't mind this kind of welcome at all." His gaze found Deborah's. "Sorry I'm late. I had to stop by the diner and let Samuel and Gertie know I won't be able to help them finish the expansion."

The warmth she saw in him made it a struggle to keep her feelings in check, but she must for Thad's sake. And for her own. She couldn't lose her heart to Eben. It would only be broken when he left.

"Are you hungry?" she cleared her throat and asked. He seemed distracted by something. Perhaps there was news on Benson. She wanted to ask, but it would have to wait until Thad went to bed.

When he smiled, some of the worry disappeared. "Starving. Samuel invited me to eat with them, but I told him no. I didn't want to miss out on one of your dinners."

She turned away, a little too pleased by his compliment. "We finished earlier, but I saved you a plate."

"Denki. I'll just go wash up. Then we need to get our chores done like we promised your Mamm," he told Thad as they went inside.

Lucy slipped on her jacket. "Now that you're back, I'm going to check outside while you eat. I'll probably touch base with the other agents while I'm out."

Eben nodded and went to wash up. Thad followed him, chatting about his day while Deborah put the plate of shepherd's pie on the table along with a glass of milk.

When Eben came into the kitchen, his face broke into a smile. "Shepherd's pie. My grandmother used to make this especially for me." He sat down at the table and Thad slid into the chair close to him.

Deborah was touched by the love in her son's eyes as he gazed at the man at their table.

"Will you join us?" Eben asked her.

How could she refuse? Then again, did she even want to refuse? She nodded and sank down into her chair.

Eben bowed his head. She did the same, motioning for Thad to follow. He whispered "Amen" and dug into the meal, closing his eyes with enjoyment. "This is so good. As good as my Grossmammi's, may she forgive me for saying so. Your Mamm is an amazing cook." He winked at Thad.

"Ja, she is," Thad eagerly agreed.

Eben grinned and ruffled the boy's hair, then finished his food and took his plate to the sink.

"Nay, I will wash the plate," Deborah insisted. "You must be tired."

"Nonsense. My grandmother taught me the value of cleaning up after myself."

Deborah couldn't help but smile. "She sounds like a wise woman."

"She was."

Once he'd finished cleaning his dish, Eben headed for the door. "Oke, Thad, we have work to do, and then I have a present for you."

Thad's face lit up. "What is it?"

"A surprise. Chores first."

Thad could barely control his curiosity, but he didn't argue as he put on his coat.

"We'll be right back," Eben said, a smile lifting the corners of his mouth.

The door closed behind them. Breath seeped from her body. Deborah sank into the rocker near the fire. Her hands shaking. Her heart racing. Peace evaded her. She was falling in love with Eben, and she didn't know how to stop it. Their lives were much too different. She could never leave her faith, and she wasn't some young girl anxious for a boy to court her. She had Thad to think about.

She held her hands close to the fire, but the chill inside her reached so deep that no amount of heat could dispel it. Staring into the fire for the longest time, she wondered how she and Thad would ever get by without Eben in their lives.

Outside, voices drifted her way, her son asking his endless questions and Eben chuckling at the boy's excitement.

"Let's go show your Mamm." Eben's voice sent a shiver down her spine.

Deborah drew in a breath and braced herself to face him again. The door opened and Thad raced to her side.

"Mamm, look what Eben gave me!" He held up a book. "It's about sledding."

Deborah took the book from Thad and admired it. "That was nice of him. Did you thank him?"

"Several times, as I recall," Eben said, smiling at the boy.

"Can I go to my room and read it?" He bounced on his toes in anticipation.

The desire to keep her son close as a buffer between them was strong, but she had no legitimate reason to do so. "Oke, but take off your coat first."

Eben sat down next to her.

"Denki. He loves the book already," she said without looking at him. She could feel him watching her. This was dangerous. She cast about for something to talk about. "How did your search for Henry go?"

He shifted in his seat. "Not well. We searched every single one of his former properties. There's no sign anyone has been there for a while. I'm worried, Deborah. We need Henry to convict Benson. Without him we have nothing."

Her thoughts went to Thad. She couldn't ask him to relive his Daed's death.

Eben clasped her hand and seemed to read her mind. "I won't let them make Thad testify. We'll find another way to bring Benson in."

She swallowed deep. Eben was a *gut* man. "I am grateful to you."

He smiled, then released her hand and sat back, his expression pensive. "I still can't help but believe I'm missing something important connected to Peter's coat." He rubbed his temples. "Let's go through it from the beginning. Do you remember where your husband bought the coat?"

Deborah thought back to that time. "He didn't. He came home wearing it one day, and when I asked him about it, he just said someone gave it to him."

"You have no idea who?"

"No, I'm sorry. He never said."

"We're missing something. Do you mind if I look at it again?"

"No, of course not. I will get it." She rose to her feet, grateful for an excuse to put space between them. Dark thoughts assailed her. There would be a day when Eben was no longer part of her life. She'd been so foolish to fall in love with him.

Outside Thad's room, Deborah drew in a deep breath, trying to compose herself. Opening the door, she went inside, hoping Thad wouldn't see her inner turmoil. Her son sat on his bed reading the book Eben had given him. He glanced up.

"I need to borrow your coat for a little while again," she said, forcing a smile. "Go back to reading your book."

Thad didn't question why. She kissed his forehead, picked up the coat, and then left the room.

The coat was a simple one, similar to others Amish men wore in this part of the country. She couldn't imagine its importance. Steeling herself, she returned to the great room and handed it to Eben. He placed it on the floor and carefully ran his fingers around the inside of the garment. When he reached one of the pockets, he stopped and brought the coat closer.

"I can't believe I missed this. There's something in here." He held it up to her.

"What do you think it is?" she asked.

Eben shook his head. "I don't know, but it just might be what Benson is so willing to kill for."

"There's a second lining in this particular pocket." He examined the opposing pocket. It wasn't nearly as thick. "I'll need to cut it out."

Deborah didn't hesitate. "Of course. I will get a knife." She hurried to the kitchen and brought one back.

Eben carefully cut through the lining to gain access to the object. He pulled out a piece of paper and unfolded it. "It looks like a map of some type." Eben handed it to Deborah. "Do you recognize the location?" he asked.

She studied the paper for a moment. "I'm not sure. It's a very basic map. It could be almost anywhere around here."

"What are you two doing?" Lucy asked, surprising them both. Neither had heard her come in.

"We found this inside Thad's coat," Eben held up the paper. "It's a map."

"You're kidding. That's odd." Lucy took the map from Eben. "Do you know the location?" she asked and Eben shook his head. "I'll take a photo and send it to Brian. If it's okay with you, I'd like to take a crack at pinpointing the place."

"I have no problem with it." Eben glanced at Deborah. "I'm sorry for destroying the lining."

She examined the damage. "You didn't. I can stitch it up easily enough."

His gaze swept over Deborah's face and came to rest on her lips. There was so much more he wanted to say to her, but with Lucy watching them, it would have to wait for another time. Clearing his throat, he rose to his feet. "It's getting late. I'll do a perimeter check before I go to bed."

"Good night," Lucy said, then took the map to the kitchen to photograph.

Eben headed for the entrance, pleased Deborah had come with him. He swiveled to face her. "Try to get some rest. I'll see you in the morning." As their gazes met, something yawned widely in his chest. He was losing his heart to her and there wasn't a thing he could do to stop it.

He didn't want to stop it.

"Good night, Deborah," he said softly. He boldly squeezed her hand, wishing he could do more than just say good night to her. Instead, he stepped back and waited while she closed the door and locked it.

After making his rounds, Eben was halfway to the barn when his cell phone rang. The number of one of the agents working with him appeared on the screen.

"I have news," Tony said. "We got permission to review some surveillance tapes taken outside of an Amish bakery in Alamosa. The owner found out what was happening and wanted to help."

"And?" Eben prompted, realizing Tony wouldn't have called unless they'd found something.

"His camera caught an argument between Benson and Yoder shortly after Peter Albrecht's death, back before Yoder changed his name from Zachary. There's no sound, but Yoder was facing the camera, so we've been able to piece together some of the conversation by reading his lips. It appears Yoder told Benson he wanted out, and if he didn't let him, he had enough evidence to put Benson away for a long time."

"We already knew that."

"Yeah, but get this. Yoder patted his coat while he was talking about evidence. Eben, it looks like the same one Peter Albrecht owned. There has to be something hidden in that coat."

"There is." Eben informed him about the map. He understood its significance now. "We need to find the location indicated on the map. It may lead to evidence that will convict Benson of money laundering and maybe even the murder of Peter Albrecht. We need answers and we need them now."

"Right, sir." Tony hung up.

Questions sped through Eben's mind. Had Benson given up on finding out what Henry had hidden in the coat and instead took the man captive to force him into handing over the evidence? With how long Henry had been missing, they might already be too late.

14

Saturday morning dawned clear, without a cloud in the sky. It was the first day without snow in over a week and perfect for their sledding trip. Deborah was grateful. Sledding was all Thad had talked about for days. She prayed Eben wouldn't disappoint her son.

Since they'd found the map, they barely saw him anymore. He left right after the morning chores and came home well after dinner was finished. She still set a plate for him each day, although at times, Thad had already gone to bed when he returned.

"When will he be here? He promised." Thad's hopeful face was pressed against the window. "I can't wait to try out my sled since Eben fixed it!"

Deborah finished preparing sandwiches for their picnic lunch, then poured cocoa into a thermos.

"Breakfast is almost ready, Thad. Eben will be here when he can." She didn't have the heart to tell the boy Eben might be too busy searching for Henry to keep his promise.

"There he is!" Thad exclaimed and hurried outside before Deborah could stop him.

"To tell you the truth, I'm surprised he's able to take the time off. The case is heating up," Lucy said.

Deborah felt guilty for taking Eben from his work.

Thad dragged Eben into the house with such eagerness that Eben barely managed to close the door, chuckling.

"Have you seen the sky this morning?" Eben asked Deborah, his eyes sparkling and bluer than ever. "This is going to be a perfect day for sledding. Almost as if Gött prepared it especially for us."

Once everyone was seated, they bowed their heads and she poured out her troubled heart in prayer. *Gött, please give us a* gut *day today. And help Eben to catch this man and bring Henry home safely.*

"Amen," Eben said for them, and they dug into the food.

"Do we have to do the chores before we go?" Thad asked with his mouth full.

Eben nodded. "Ja, we have to do our chores first. Poor Cinnamon would be very uncomfortable if we didn't milk her. And I'm pretty sure all the animals would be mad if we failed to feed them. Why, the chickens might go on strike, and then we wouldn't have these delicious eggs tomorrow."

Thad giggled and shoved a spoonful of eggs into his mouth.

"Are you sure you can take the time off right now?" Deborah asked. "I know you are busy."

The affection in his eyes swept her breath away. It promised so much, yet she couldn't allow that hope to take root.

"There are plenty of other agents working the case today. And don't worry about Benson. I've asked a couple of my men to come along with us to keep watch while we're having fun." He grinned at Thad before asking, "You're coming too, aren't you?"

While her head urged her to refuse—keep her distance from Eben and the future pain he represented—her heart wouldn't let her say no. She longed to be with him and was looking forward to the day almost as much as Thad.

"Ja," she whispered.

"I hoped you would," he said softly. "All right, let's get a move on, Thad. It'll be daylight soon."

When they returned after completing the chores, Eben said, "I thought it best if we took the buggy. I don't think my car will make it through the deep snow around back. The other agents will follow behind in their car."

"Are you ready, Mamm?" Thad asked, holding the sled in his arms.

She handed Eben the picnic basket and the thermos of hot cocoa. "Ja, let's go." She donned her cloak and traveling bonnet and stepped outside.

Lucy waved to them. "Have fun. I'll call you if anything comes up."

Thad put the sled behind the seat, then scrambled up on the bench while Eben lifted the basket up to him. She clasped Eben's hand and let him help her into the buggy. His touch was strong, warm, and filled with promises she couldn't let herself accept.

When they were all settled, Deborah shook the reins and the mare headed forward with the car following a little more slowly.

"Thad has told me all the kids in the community use the hills behind your home to sled."

The cold air stung her cheeks, yet she was happy to be sharing this experience with Eben. "That's right."

"I can't wait to try out my sled. I bet it's even faster now!" Thad exclaimed, his eyes alight.

Deborah couldn't help but get caught up in Thad's excitement. "I remember sledding down those hills when I was a child."

She stopped the buggy close to the first hill and Eben hopped down. Before she knew what was happening, his hands circled her waist and he lifted her down. She drew in a quick breath, wishing she could slow her pulse. Holding her longer than was strictly necessary, he searched her eyes. If only she could read his thoughts. He let her go and she stepped back, able to breathe again.

Deborah turned away and tried to reclaim her composure while Eben and Thad discussed which hill to test first. Finally, they agreed on one and trudged through thick snow until they reached the top of the hill.

"Mamm, watch me!" Thad called out.

She waved from the bottom of the hill. "I am watching."

"Lean forward when you go down and if you fall over, make sure you let go of the reins." She heard Eben say. "Ready?"

Thad nodded eagerly, his full attention on the path in front of him.

With a gentle push from Eben, Thad went flying down the hill, whooping and laughing along the way while Deborah held her breath. She didn't want to fuss over her son, but still it worried her to see her Boppli racing down the hill at such speed.

Once he came to a stop, Thad hopped up and looked to Eben. "Did you see? I flew! This is the fastest sled ever."

"I think you're right. Want to do it again?"

Thad grabbed the sled and ran up the hill once more.

"Why don't you come up here with us?" Eben called down to her.

"Oke." She hadn't imagined having so much fun at a simple sledding outing, but watching Eben's and Thad's delight brought her more joy than she could have imagined.

"Wait here," he told Thad and hurried down to her. "Here, let me help you up. It's a little slippery." He clasped her hand in his, and she told herself he was just being a gentleman. Still, childish pleasure swept through her as they headed up the hill together holding hands.

"Are you okay?" Eben studied her. "You're not too cold?"

"I'm fine," she said, aware that she wore a smile that stretched from ear to ear.

"All right, Thad, let's show your Mamm how it's done."

Thad braced himself, and Eben gave him a push. The boy flew down the side of the hill, laughing the whole way down.

"He really is having fun." Deborah brushed a strand of hair from her face, smiling up at Eben. "Denki for this. I know you've been busy with the case, but I am grateful to you for making time for him." Her smile faded as his eyes captured her.

"I'd do anything for him—and you," he whispered.

She was thankful when Thad returned just then. Her chest was tight.

Thad spent the rest of the morning sliding down the hills. He even got Eben to go down a couple of times.

"Oke, let's take a break for lunch," Eben said when Thad hauled the sled back up around noon.

"Aw, do we have to?"

"Yes, we do. Your Mamm has prepared something delicious for us. We should enjoy it. Aren't you hungry?"

"I am," Thad admitted.

Eben cleared away the snow on a large boulder before setting their basket on top. He took out the sandwiches and macaroni salad while Deborah poured cocoa for everyone. The two agents accompanying them took their plates to the car to eat while keeping a careful eye on the surrounding countryside.

"Thank you." Eben smiled his appreciation as he accepted a warm cup from her, and she smiled back.

Thad was wolfing down his sandwich, eager to get back to sledding.

"Slow down," Deborah urged, placing a hand on his arm. "Food is meant to be enjoyed."

The boy nodded but barely slowed down.

While they ate, Eben's cell phone rang. "Excuse me." He stepped away to take the call.

When he returned, the taut set of his jaw told her he hadn't gotten good news.

"That was Lucy. We have a spotting of Benson and Henry at one of Benson's storage facilities near Alamosa. I'm sorry, Thad, but I have to go."

Thad's face fell and Deborah tugged her son close. "It is oke, Eben. We understand you have a job to do."

"I'm afraid we have to get going. Lucy is waiting for us. I'll just go have a word with the other agents first."

He stepped away. While Deborah gathered the remains of their meal, Thad slogged over to get his sled, tears in his eyes.

She gently chucked him under the chin. "I know you're disappointed, but we've had a fun morning, and Eben is trying to keep us safe, so dry your eyes. We don't want him to feel bad."

Thad sniffled and wiped his face. "Ja, Mamm."

When Eben returned, he knelt in front of the boy. "How about as soon as this case is over, we come back and do some more sledding? This time, no interruptions. We'll sled all day if it's okay with your Mamm."

"Ja!" Thad threw his arms around Eben's neck and hugged him. Over the top of the boy's head, his eyes sought hers. As much as she wanted to believe there would be a next time, she didn't, and it broke her heart. Why would Eben make a promise he couldn't keep?

"Be careful please," Deborah whispered after they drove home and were settled inside the house.

Eben glanced past her to where Lucy, sitting by the woodstove, feigned interest in Thad's sledding book. "Don't worry, I'll be fine. Just take care of Thad and yourself." He squeezed her hand, his gaze lingering before he reluctantly let her go. "I will see you soon." Resisting the urge to kiss her proved nearly impossible. Instead, he opened the door and stepped outside into the winter day.

Once he climbed into the car, he called Adam to check in. "Anything new?" Eben drove away, his heart heavy with regret.

"Nope. We have the unit surrounded. No one's come in or out since the sighting. We're waiting on you before we breach."

"I'll be there as soon as I can." Eben ended the call and accelerated.

Throughout the drive, all he could think about was Deborah. He loved her. There was no doubt. And he loved Thad. Yet so many things stood in their way. Barely a year had passed since Peter's death. Deborah still mourned her husband. How could he ask for her love when she still grieved? And he wasn't sure he would be accepted back into the Amish community. If not, where did that leave them?

Shoving aside the pain that seemed to smother him these days, he hit the outskirts of Alamosa and drove to the storage unit. He parked behind one of the dozen or so vehicles staged there.

Adam spotted him and came over. "There's been no sign of movement. I don't like it."

Eben didn't either. "Let's get in there." He drew his weapon.

One of the agents lifted the door. Flashlight beams bounced around the empty unit. No one had been there in a while.

Frustrated, Eben ran a hand through his hair. "Where'd the tip come from?"

"Anonymous. A woman called it in but wouldn't give her name," Adam confirmed.

Eben thought it sounded an awful lot like a setup, but they had to check every tip. "If the call's legit and Benson was here with Henry, then there's still a chance that Henry is alive. But something about this doesn't feel right." He gestured toward the empty storage unit. "Someone's playing with us. But why?"

15

Deborah had looked forward to Faith's wedding since the day the young woman had come into her shop and asked for her help.

Bishop Timothy had granted Lucy permission to attend the service to protect Deborah and Thad. The three-hour ceremony would begin at eight thirty in the morning, with guests invited to stay for the midday meal and then dinner.

Deborah loved weddings. They were such a special time. The focus on friends and family was part of what made the Amish community such a tight-knit group.

After hitching Bridget to the buggy, Deborah led the mare around to the front of the house where Lucy and Thad waited.

"It will be a great day for a wedding. But do they have to start so early?" Lucy asked with a laugh as she climbed up next to Thad.

Deborah grinned. "Be glad you are not part of the wedding party. You would have been helping with the activities by four in the morning."

"What? Why can't you Amish do things the Englisch way, or at least on our timetable?"

"Trust me, Amish weddings are a special event." Deborah headed the mare toward the Wengerd home where the wedding would take place.

In preparation, each room of the family home would have been scrubbed until it gleamed, even painted if necessary.

On the drive over, Deborah recalled her own wedding, then followed her memories back to when Peter had begun to court her. The

San Luis Valley youth attended singings at the homes where church services were held. It was at one of these gatherings that Peter first caught her eye. Though she'd known him since childhood, it wasn't until that evening that she noticed he'd grown into a handsome, but a shy young man with shaggy brown hair and dark eyes that lit up whenever he saw her. Peter had asked to drive her home. She'd fallen in love with him right away. They'd both been so excited about their future together.

Deborah brought the buggy to a stop behind a group of other buggies. Jeremiah Lapp, a newlywed himself, waited as they climbed down. He would be responsible for taking care of Bridget during the wedding.

"Grossdaddi and Grossmammi!" Thad darted to meet Matthew and Elizabeth, who beamed at him.

Deborah followed and introduced Lucy to her in-laws.

Matthew bowed his head. "It is *gut* to meet you, Lucy. A fine day for a wedding." He nodded in approval. Deborah and Lucy fell into step beside them while Thad ran ahead, barely containing his excitement.

"It is indeed," Deborah said, remembering her own wedding day. The weather had been crisp and clear, much like today.

Lucy glanced around at the crowd of people gathering. "How many people normally attend these things?"

Lucy was concerned about protecting them, of course, but Deborah never felt safer than among the people of her community. "Most everyone, along with the bride and groom's extended families. It could be close to three hundred, even though we are a small district."

"That's a lot of people. I need you and Thad to stay close to me, okay?"

When they entered the house, the usher directed the women to the right side of the room. Deborah spotted Gertie seated a few rows up and slipped in next to her, while Matthew and Thad sat on the benches at the left side, as they would for the biweekly church service.

When all the guests were seated, a deacon stood before the crowd and led them in hymns from the *Ausbund*, while the minister counseled Faith and Amos in another part of the house.

Deborah thought about the day she and Peter had stood before the minister and answered his questions about marriage. It had been a solemn yet beautiful experience, and a memory she treasured, as she treasured all her memories with Peter.

Out of the corner of her eye, Deborah spotted Faith slip onto the bench up front along with Amos and the minister. After the last hymn finished, the minister rose and took his place at the front of the room to lead the congregation in a prayer.

When the prayer ended, the minister spoke of the Amish belief that marriage vows were a promise made to Gött and not simply to each other. He spoke of the sanctity of marriage and the importance of the married couple putting Gött first in everything. Deborah's thoughts drifted back to the time when she'd made her vows to Peter. Faith's face glowed with joy, a joy Deborah remembered wistfully.

When the sermon concluded, the minister asked Faith and Amos to step forward from their seats in preparation for the vows.

"Faith, will you remain with Amos until death?" the minister asked in a somber tone.

"I will," Faith replied, her eyes sparkling and her voice strong.

"And will you be loyal and care for Amos during adversity, affliction, sickness, and weakness?"

Faith glanced at Amos, her eyes shining. "I will."

He repeated the same vows to Amos. Then, taking the couple's hands in his, he wished them the blessing and mercy of Gött. "Go forth in Gött's name. You are now Mann and Fraa."

With a final prayer, the ceremony drew to a close. Then, in a rush of activity, the men put together the benches used in the service to form tables. The women hurried to the kitchen to lend a hand with the meal.

"I'm not sure what to do," Lucy whispered to Deborah, a perplexed expression on her face.

"Just follow me and do what I do, oke? It will all be well."

The corner table was reserved for the bride and groom and the bridal party, with the unmarried boys seated opposite the girls.

When the white tablecloths were in place, the women carried out roasted chicken with stuffing, mashed potatoes and gravy, creamed celery, coleslaw, applesauce, cherry pie, fruit salad, tapioca pudding, and bread, along with butter and various jellies prepared by the women in the family.

When it was their time to eat, Deborah and Gertie filled their plates while Lucy kept a close eye on Thad.

"Such a beautiful wedding," Gertie said with a hint of reminiscence in her tone.

Deborah sighed. "Ja. I guess all married women think about their wedding day on an occasion like this."

"I think you are right." Gertie hesitated then asked, "How is Eben? Samuel and I miss seeing him each day."

Deborah desperately needed to talk to her friend about her feelings. "He is fine."

Gertie placed her hand over Deborah's. "And how are you?"

All the secrets of her heart poured out while tears threatened to spill from her eyes. When Deborah finished, she waited for Gertie to say something. Her friend didn't appear surprised to hear Eben was an FBI agent.

"You knew?" Deborah asked in surprise.

Gertie nodded. "Eben came by the diner and told us what

happened." She squeezed Deborah's hand. "I've seen how close you and he are becoming. He's an honorable man, Deborah. He told us he wants to return to his Amish roots, but he doesn't think it possible. I urged him to pray about it. Gött will supply the answers he needs."

Deborah was shocked. Eben had talked about returning to his roots? Hope took flight in her heart, yet she forced it down. Even if he chose to return to the Amish life, that didn't mean it would be here in the San Luis Valley, and it certainly didn't mean he wanted it to be with her.

After the food was cleared away, the young people had their singing while the community members socialized. Spending the day with friends soothed her troubled heart and lifted her spirits.

Once the evening meal finished, the wedding activities drew to a close.

"Ah, Samuel is ready to leave. Why don't you and Lucy stop by and have lunch with us tomorrow?" Gertie suggested.

"We will." Deborah hugged Gertie tight, then waved at Samuel. It was getting late and time for them to head home as well. She scanned the room for Lucy, but the younger woman was nowhere in sight. Fear crept up her spine. Frantic, she hurried to the last place she'd seen Thad playing with David.

"Were you looking for me?" Lucy appeared at her side, her face flushed.

"Where were you? You had me worried."

"I'm sorry. I wanted to take a look around outside before we left. Are you ready to go?"

Deborah nodded. "Ja, it is getting late. I'll go find Thad." Lucy came with her. After looking everywhere, Deborah found Thad standing in the corner by himself. She could tell something had upset him. Kneeling in front of him, she grasped his shoulders. "What is wrong? Did something happen?"

Thad wouldn't look at her. "Nay, nothing is wrong. I just want to go home."

Perhaps he and David argued. She'd ask him again after a *gut* night's sleep. Gripping his hand in hers, she said, "Let's go say goodbye to your grandparents." Elizabeth gathered with a group of ladies talking, and Deborah got her attention.

"Are you leaving?" Elizabeth asked.

She nodded. "It is getting late and Thad is tired."

Elizabeth hugged her grandson tight. "You will come see us soon?"

Deborah assured her they would stop by following the next church service.

After saying goodbye to Matthew, they headed out into the darkness.

The young man tending to Bridget harnessed the mare to the buggy and brought it over.

With Thad sandwiched between them, Deborah urged the mare toward home while her son leaned heavily against her. "Are you feeling okay?" she asked.

Thad barely nodded, the reaction so unlike his usual energetic self.

By the time they reached the house, Thad had fallen asleep against her. She shook him gently. "We're home," she said when he glanced around, confused.

Eben must have been watching for them. As soon as the buggy pulled up in front of the house, he hurried out carrying a lantern. "How was the wedding?" he asked.

Lucy hopped down first. "Good, though different than what I expected. Thad fell asleep on the ride home."

"Too much fun, huh?" Eben grinned up at Thad.

The boy jumped down without answering and ran inside the house.

Lucy followed with a shrug.

Eben helped Deborah down. "What was that about?" he asked.

She let go of a breath. "I wish I knew. He's been like that since right before we came home." Something had scared Thad, much like the time when he'd forgotten his coat. It worried her to think Thad had kept something as terrifying as watching his father get pushed from the roof to himself for so long. What else did he keep secret? She wasn't sure how much more her precious son could stand.

"Did something happen at the wedding?" Eben pressed, the worry in her eyes troubling him.

"Not as far as I noticed. Thad spent most of the afternoon playing with David and his other friends. He appeared to be having fun, and Lucy kept a close watch over him. But when the time came to leave, I found him standing by himself. Eben, he was terrified." She shivered. "I asked him what happened, but he wouldn't talk to me. And he barely said two words on the ride home. I'm worried about him." She peered up at him, pleading with her eyes. "He opened up to you once before. Would you speak with him again?"

He didn't hesitate. "Of course."

"Did you find Henry?" she asked as they headed toward the house.

He shook his head. "I have agents searching every square inch of Alamosa. I'm heading back there tonight to help with the search. I just wanted to see you first." He shouldn't have said it, but he couldn't help himself.

She swallowed. He touched her cheek, and her eyes drifted closed. More than anything, he wanted to take her in his arms and kiss her until the case and the danger and their different lives and even time itself melted into nothing. But too many things stood in the way.

When he opened the door for her, Eben looked deep into her eyes. Unable to stop himself, he leaned down and brushed a quick kiss across her lips. He was sure his heart stopped for the moment their lips touched.

She gaped at him, then gave him a small smile. He brushed a thumb across her cheek, and together they went inside. He knew no words needed to be spoken. They both understood their situation perfectly.

Lucy and Thad sat next to the fire. Lucy talked quietly to the boy, who stared into the fire without answering.

When Eben closed the door, Lucy rose to her feet, shaking her head, and slipped outside to do the nightly rounds.

While Deborah made coffee in the kitchen, Eben knelt in front of the boy. "Did something happen to upset you at the wedding?" he asked gently. Thad didn't look at him. "You can tell me if it did. You can tell me anything, you know. You won't get in trouble. We just want to know if you're okay."

Tears filled Thad's eyes, and he jumped to his feet. "Nothing happened!" he shouted. "And I don't want to talk about it." He ran to his room and slammed the door.

Eben slowly rose to his feet. He hated that he'd made the boy cry.

Deborah handed him a cup of coffee. "You did everything you could. Thad can be stubborn."

"We'll figure it out. Try not to worry too much. It could be nothing. To be safe, I think you and Thad should stay home tomorrow." Eben couldn't explain it, but he had a feeling everything would soon come to a head, for better or worse.

He took a sip of coffee. "I wish I didn't have to leave again." His place was here by her side—protecting her and the boy who'd won his heart, but he had orders and he was sworn to obey them.

"I wish that too," she said, so quietly he almost didn't hear her.

He washed and dried his cup, then set it back in the cupboard. "I'd better go. I'll speak with Lucy first. Maybe she noticed something more than she realized. Come lock the door behind me." As she stood close to him to let him out of the house, there were so many things he wanted to say to her. He prayed for the right time to tell her all the secrets of his heart.

When Deborah slid the door locks into place, he clicked on the flashlight and headed behind the house, where he discovered Lucy talking on her phone.

She noticed him coming and ended the call. "That was Stephens. Everything is quiet at his post. He and his partner checked around the area. There's no sign of Benson. Do you think he's still hanging around? With all the manpower around, he'd be a fool to try anything."

Eben flicked off the flashlight. "Maybe, but Benson has a lot to lose, so he's probably willing to take greater risks. Especially if Thad saw him murder Peter." He hadn't meant to tell Deborah's secret, but it slipped out.

Lucy gasped. "He didn't!"

Eben told her everything and asked her to keep the information out of the files. "We don't want to make him testify. No one should have to relive something like that."

"Poor little guy. I can't imagine keeping that burden inside." With a shake of her head, she said, "I should head back in." She'd taken only a few steps when Eben remembered what he wanted to speak with her about.

"Hang on a second. Did you notice anything odd happening with Thad today at the wedding?"

Lucy thought about it for a minute. "Now that you mention it, I think I saw him arguing with his friend. You know how kids are."

"But nothing else?" Eben couldn't let go of the feeling that there was something more.

She looked thoughtful, then said, "No, nothing. I'll see you tomorrow." She waved and went into the house.

Eben unlocked his car door and slid in. With his thoughts unsettled, he called his commander.

"Everything okay there?" Brian asked by way of greeting.

Eben had no proof of anything out of the ordinary. "Yes. Just a bad vibe, I guess. I can't help but think Benson is close by. Have the tech guys come up with anything on the map yet?" They desperately needed a break in this case.

"What map are you talking about?" Brian asked, sounding puzzled. "I haven't heard anything about it."

"The map we found in Albrecht's coat," Eben said, his confusion mirroring his commander's. "Lucy was going to send you pictures of it." He couldn't believe Lucy had failed to let Brian know about a key piece of evidence.

"She probably took the initiative and is trying to pinpoint the location herself using our methods and technology. You know Lucy is a genius when it comes to ferreting out information."

"I'm sure you're right." Still, Eben wasn't convinced. "I've got more guys on the search for Benson. I'm going back there now. Hopefully, we'll flush him out soon."

Ending the call, Eben focused on the road ahead. As much as he wanted to find Benson, his thoughts centered on Deborah. He longed to call her his own, to make a life with her. The last thing he wanted was to leave her for good once the case ended.

But did he have a choice?

16

"Why can't I go to school today?" Thad asked for the third time that morning.

"Because Eben thinks it best if we stay home," Deborah said. So far, every attempt at getting him to talk about what happened at the wedding had been met with a sullen shake of his head. She wondered if a day of sledding might cheer him up.

She waited until he was distracted before pulling Lucy aside. "Do you think it would be okay if we took Thad sledding again? He could use some fun."

Lucy seemed surprised by the request. "Oh, I don't know. I'll need a word with my boss first."

While Lucy made the call, Deborah finished clearing away the remains of breakfast. Sleep had eluded her the night before. Her worry for Thad was foremost in her thoughts, but every time she closed her eyes, Eben's handsome face appeared before her. Remembering his kiss warmed her cheeks. He'd come to occupy much of her thoughts each day. She was losing her heart to him—perhaps had already lost it completely, which would only lead to grief when he left.

"We've got the go-ahead to sled," Lucy came into the kitchen and announced.

Letting go of her heartache seemed impossible, but she would try for Thad's sake. "Denki, Lucy. I'll tell Thad."

She went to Thad's room. The boy was reading the book Eben

had given him. Deborah sat on the edge of the bed. "Would you like to go sledding today, Thad?"

The boy's eyes grew large, and he jumped up and hugged her tight. "Ja, Mamm! Can Eben come with us?"

She had anticipated the question. How could she not, when she knew how important Eben was to her son? "I'm afraid not. He has to work, but Lucy is going with us. Go get your sled. I'll make us some lunch to take along."

She quickly put together sandwiches with Lucy's help.

"Mamm, I'm ready." Thad stood in the foyer, his coat on and the sled leaning against the door.

Deborah chuckled at the boy's excitement. "Then let's get going."

With Thad's help, Deborah harnessed Bridget, and they headed behind the house to the hills. She stopped the buggy, and Thad hopped down then raced up the hill.

"Be careful!" Deborah called after him.

"I will, Mamm!" the boy hollered over his shoulder.

"He really loves sledding, doesn't he?" Lucy said. Together they watched Thad make pass after pass down the hill.

For a little while, Deborah let go of her cares and simply soaked up Thad's happiness.

At one point, he hurried up to her. "Can I go down that hill?" he asked pointing to one of the bigger ones.

"Oh, I don't know. That looks pretty steep."

"I'll be okay, Mamm. Can I?"

The boy was growing up quickly, and she didn't want to be overprotective. "Oke, but be careful."

With a whoop, he ran toward the hill before she could change her mind.

She lost sight of him when he reached the top of the hill. Her pulse sped. Drawing in a breath, she waited, but Thad didn't reappear. "Where is he?" she whispered shakily.

"I don't know." Lucy frowned and gazed at the spot where Thad disappeared.

Deborah rushed up the hill with Lucy close behind. The snow grabbed at her feet, adding to the nightmarish quality that had suddenly stolen the day. When they reached the top, there was only white in every direction.

Thad was gone.

"Thad, where are you?" she screamed. There was no answer, only a set of footprints in the snow. "Lucy, look."

"I see them. Wait here." Lucy drew her weapon and followed the prints.

Deborah had never felt so helpless before. She didn't know what to do. "Thad, where are you?" she called out.

But there was only silence.

Eben pulled up in front of Deborah's home and got out. He had just started for the door when the noise of someone screaming froze him in place. It was Deborah calling for Thad, the panic in her tone clear.

Eben sprinted toward the sound of her voice.

He'd called off the search near Alamosa. He was positive the tip had been a hoax to draw their attention away from Deborah and Thad. For the entire trip back, Eben tried reaching Lucy, but she wasn't answering her phone.

Eben found Deborah at the top of a hill, her face wild with fear.

"Deborah, was iss letz?" He gripped her arms and forced her to look at him. He had a horrible guess about what was going on, but he desperately wanted to be wrong.

"Thad is gone." Her voice shook. "He wanted to sled down this hill. When he reached the top, he just disappeared. Lucy went looking for him." She drew in a breath. "Eben, this has to be Benson."

"We don't know that for sure," he tried to reassure her, but it felt as if his worst nightmare had come true. In his gut, he knew Benson had taken Thad.

Taking out his phone, he called one of the men guarding Deborah's house. He needed immediate backup. "Stephens, it's Eben. I need you over here now." He gave the location, then glanced at Deborah. "We think Benson may have Thad. Lucy is following a set of footprints."

Stephens's silence was confusing.

"Did you hear me, Stephens?"

"I did, but we're actually in Alamosa. All of us. Lucy told us there'd been a new sighting of Benson here. She said you wanted all hands on deck."

Eben couldn't believe what he heard. Why would Lucy do such a thing?

Unless . . .

Suddenly all the little things about her clicked together in his head—her strange secretiveness, the fact that she hadn't told Brian about the map, and countless other things he'd ignored at the time—forming one complete and terrible picture.

Lucy had been working with Benson all along. The realization struck like a blow to the chest.

"The search near Alamosa is a bust. Get here pronto." Eben disconnected the call and struggled not to show Deborah his reaction. "I need you to wait here. Backup is on the way. When they arrive, tell them which way I've gone." He started to follow the footsteps, but she grabbed his arm.

The fear in her eyes scared him. "Eben, I can't lose him," she whispered, her lips trembling.

He squeezed her hand. "You won't. I'll find him."

Eben followed the tracks, the path leading him straight to a cave at the base of the mountains. It dawned on him this could be the location marked on the map.

Eben quickly called Stephens again, giving GPS coordinates from his phone.

"We're ten minutes out. Any sign of Lucy or the boy?"

Eben didn't share his revelation or his fears. "Nothing yet. Hurry."

He ended the call and eased inside the cave. When his eyes adjusted to the dim light, he couldn't believe what he saw.

A man stood close to Thad, who was curled up on the ground, sniffling. The man whirled at the sound of Eben's footsteps.

Benson.

Lucy stood next to him with a smug sneer on her face. It was clear Lucy was Benson's willing partner. Henry Yoder, appearing badly injured, huddled in the corner of the cave.

Benson snatched Thad up and pressed the barrel of a gun to his head. "Don't come any closer if you want the boy to live."

Eben froze. He couldn't believe any of this was happening—and it was even worse that it was because one of his own agents was dirty.

"How could you do this, Lucy?" he asked, unable to grasp the depth of her deceit.

Lucy smiled at his confusion. "Because I love him and he loves me. I wasn't about to let you put him in jail."

The reality of Lucy's betrayal hit hard. "You've been feeding Benson information about the investigation all along."

Lucy lifted her chin. "That's right. I had to draw your attention away from the house so Victor could grab the boy. We can't let him stop us. He knows too much."

Realization dawned hard. "You called in the tip."

"Of course," Lucy said matter-of-factly.

"Shut your mouth!" Benson barked at Lucy, his face burning with rage. Without warning, he aimed the gun at Lucy and pulled the trigger.

She dropped to the ground, gripping her leg. "You shot me?" she gasped, the smirk replaced by a twisted grimace of pain.

Benson turned the gun back on Thad. "I don't need you blabbing everything to him." He glared at Eben. "Don't try anything, Fed. Me and this kid are going to walk out of here nice and easy."

There was no time to wait for backup. If Benson got Thad out of the cave, he'd kill the boy to silence him.

Thad's terrified gaze latched onto Eben.

"It's going to be okay," Eben assured him. "You remember what I told you?" He prayed the boy remembered.

"Shut up!" Benson ordered. He gestured with the gun. "Get away from the opening."

"Now, Thad!" Eben yelled.

Thad stomped down hard on Benson's foot. The man yelped in pain and loosened his grip. The boy yanked his arm free and made a run for the opening.

Before Benson could react, Eben charged forward and tackled him to the cave floor. Benson was strong and determined. It took several minutes and all of Eben's efforts to finally subdue the man.

Forcing his arms behind his back, Eben cuffed him.

Lucy hobbled to her feet, dragging her injured leg.

"Stay where you are," Eben warned her. "I'll restrain you if I have to."

She ignored him. "You told me you loved me!" she yelled at Benson. "But you shot me."

"Keep your mouth shut," Benson growled. "Don't you dare tell him anything."

Lucy glared at him. "I won't keep quiet. I should never have listened to you. I risked everything for you. Well, you're going to pay for ruining my life. I'm going to tell them everything. Everything, you hear me?"

She lunged for Benson, but Eben blocked her way. "That's enough. Sit down. You shouldn't put weight on that leg."

Sinking to the ground, she covered her face with her hands and burst into tears.

Eben called for an ambulance, made sure Benson couldn't escape, and went to check on Henry. One of the man's eyes was swollen shut, and there was dried blood on his lip.

"Do you think you can stand?" Eben asked him.

"I think so." He favored his left arm and gasped when Eben took his hand to help him up. He leaned heavily on Eben. "I tried to keep him from harming the boy. I did my best."

Eben patted the man's arm. "I know you did. You were great. He won't hurt anyone ever again. With your help and Lucy's, we can put Victor Benson away for a long time."

17

Deborah charged toward the sound as soon as she heard the gunshot. She ran as fast as she could following the footprints, the cold air burning her lungs and the snow freezing her feet and legs. But with every step and every passing moment she feared she'd be too late. Just as she finally reached a cave where the footprints ended, Thad shot out of the opening.

"Mamm!"

She caught him and wrapped her arms around him tight.

As she held him close, she looked inside. Lucy sat on the ground, holding her leg. Blood seeped from a wound. The man she recognized as Benson was handcuffed. Eben stood next to Henry Yoder, who appeared beaten but alive.

Thad pointed at Lucy. "I saw her talking to that man at the wedding. She told me she would hurt you if I said anything. Please don't be mad. I didn't want to lie, but I didn't want her to hurt you." His eyes pled with her to understand.

Deborah smoothed back the boy's hair. "It's oke. You didn't do anything wrong." She felt the stab of betrayal. Lucy must have been working for Benson all along.

Thad's face crumpled. "I did so. I saw him push Daed off the roof and I was too scared to say anything. I thought he would hurt you if I told."

"Oh, my sweet boy, there was nothing you could have done to save your father. None of this is your fault. You did nothing wrong," she assured him again, then held him while his body shook with his sobs, the truth finally revealed. Relieved at her son's safety, she sent a silent prayer of thanksgiving to Gött. Benson would face justice for taking Peter from them, maybe Lucy too. But in time, she'd find a way to forgive Benson and Lucy because it was the Amish way.

Eben smiled. "You can take him home. You're both safe now. I'll go with Henry to the hospital and get his statement. We'll talk soon."

With tears in her eyes, she took Thad's hand and together they headed home through the snow, with Eben's assurances echoing in her ear. She was safe. Thad was safe.

But her heart was in danger of breaking.

Eben rode with Henry to the hospital. Lucy would be treated and taken into custody. Benson was going immediately to jail.

Once the doctor treated Henry's injuries, he stepped out into the hall and said Henry was asking for him. Eben went inside. Henry pointed to the chair near the bed and Eben sat, waiting for Henry to begin.

Henry didn't make him wait long. "I'm sorry I bailed on the FBI. When Benson got out, I asked that agent from the cave about protective custody, but she told me I had nothing to worry about. I knew Benson would be out for my blood, so I took matters into my own hands. I changed my name and came here. I had no idea you'd find me anyway, and I had no idea that agent would tell Benson where I was. I recognized you from when I cooperated with the FBI. I'd decided to give the coat back to Thad because I knew, with the FBI in town, you'd probably put an agent close to Deborah for protection."

"It was your coat all along," Eben said, figuring out the story as he spoke. "You hid the map inside and gave the coat to Peter, thinking Benson would never discover it."

"Yes, it belonged to me. I gave it to Peter for safekeeping, thinking Benson wouldn't realize it was mine." Henry blew out a sigh. "Peter came to me the day before he died and told me he'd heard Benson discussing how he'd used subpar material on several jobsites to save money. Peter wanted to confront Benson, but I warned him not to." Henry shook his head. "I think he did it anyway, and that's why Benson killed him."

"Unbelievable." Benson's criminal activities went much deeper than they'd thought.

"The day Benson killed Peter, I saw the coat lying near the worksite, so I grabbed it. I thought the coat would be safe with Thad, but then I saw him wearing it and got worried. What if Benson found out the boy had witnessed his father's death and came after him? At that point, I had no way of knowing Benson had an FBI agent working for him. I asked Thad for the coat back. I planned to turn it over to the FBI myself, but Benson showed up, and things got messy."

"Where's the evidence now?" Eben asked. He'd searched the cave from top to bottom after Henry, Benson, and Lucy had been picked up, but he hadn't found anything.

"I moved it. I was worried Benson would find it on his own, so I hid it at an abandoned farm north of town." Henry sighed deeply. "Then your agent gave the map to Benson and told him the boy had seen him killing his father. He'd tried to make me tell him where I'd hidden the evidence, but I wouldn't." He stopped for a breath and put a hand to his head, which must've ached.

Eben waited patiently for him to continue.

"Benson forced me to go to the location on the map. He said he'd kill the boy if I didn't tell him where the evidence was. Only I realized he'd kill us both anyway. He couldn't afford to leave any witnesses behind. Thank God you came along when you did. You saved my life, Agent Graber."

"I'm just glad you're okay," Eben said quietly. "Try to get some rest now. We'll talk more later."

Outside, Brian waited in the hallway. "Did you get his statement?"

"I did. He's cooperating completely." All Eben could think about were the tears he'd seen in Deborah's eyes when she'd left him at the cave. He wanted to go to her. Reassure her this life with the FBI wasn't his any longer. He wanted to be plain again.

"I'll want you to sit in on the interview with Lucy." Brian blew out a breath. "I still can't believe she did so much harm."

Eben gathered his courage. Saying the words were the hardest thing he'd ever had to do, but it was the right decision. "I'm sorry, but I can't."

Brian's brows slanted together. "Why not?"

"Because I'm done. I don't want this life anymore. I'm returning to my Amish roots right now, here in the San Juan Valley. I know it won't be easy and I have a long road ahead of me to gain the trust of the people of this community, but this is what I want."

Brian pinned him with a knowing look. "And she is what you want as well."

"If she'll have me," he said quietly, then shook Brian's hand when he offered it.

"I can't say I didn't see it coming, and I think it'll be the best thing for you, though I'll certainly miss you. Good luck," his commander and friend told him.

Eben knew luck wasn't something he could count on. Only Gött could clear his way.

The drive to Deborah's farm seemed to take forever. He'd poured his heart out to Bishop Timothy and found the answers he needed. Now, it was up to her.

When he pulled up, he could see her watching from the window. Deborah opened the door before he knocked, her expression forlorn. She appeared to be trying not to cry.

"Is Henry oke?" she asked.

"It looked worse than it was. He will be released from the hospital soon and he is fully cooperating. Lucy will too."

"So, it is over." She sounded downright forlorn about it, more so than someone who'd just found out she and her son were safe should.

His heart went out to her. "It is."

She looked away from him. "You'll be leaving then."

He gently took her hands in his, surprising her. "No, I'm not going anywhere. I'm done with this life, Deborah. I spoke to Bishop Timothy and told him everything about my past and how my father was excommunicated. The bishop says I will need to spend time living in the community, attending classes, and participating in community events for an extended period of time, as well as gaining the church members' support. He believes the community will welcome me into the fold, and he will do everything in his power to help me." He hesitated. "Will *you* accept me as a member of your community?"

Tears shimmered in her eyes.

He tipped her chin back. "I love you with all my heart, Deborah, and if you will have me as your Mann, I want very much to marry you someday."

With tears falling down her cheeks, Deborah wrapped her arms around him and held him close. "I love you, too, Eben, and I would be honored to be your Fraa. For now and for always."

Epilogue

One year later, Christmas Eve

Snow piled high outside the window and Deborah couldn't have been happier. This was her favorite time of the year. And she was in her own home with her son . . . and Eben.

She waited for Thad and Eben to finish their chores outside. Tonight, Thad would be one of the wise men in the school play. For days he'd been so excited, reciting his part for them again and again.

Christmas cards were hung around the house. Gifts for the family, wrapped in bright paper, formed a pile near the stove. She and Thad had delivered their cards to friends and family during the week.

For the past few days, Deborah had been busily cooking for the Christmas meal they would celebrate with Matthew and Elizabeth. Today, she'd baked her special cookies to take to the school program.

This would be her first Christmas as Eben's Fraa. Later, when it was just the two of them, she would tell him her news. She was expecting a child, and she was so happy. First their marriage last fall after his baptism, and now a baby. She couldn't wait to see the joy on his face.

Outside, voices carried into the kitchen. Footsteps sounded on the porch. The door opened.

"Something smells wonderful." Eben's deep voice enveloped her like a warm hug. Her Mann. After Peter's death, she couldn't have imagined being this happy again, but Gött had richly blessed her with a second chance, and a growing family.

Deborah placed the last of the cookies in the tin.

She turned and found Eben in the doorway watching her. A smile spread across his beloved face.

"Are you ready, my Fraa?" he asked, holding out his hand to her.

Taking it, Deborah planted a gentle kiss on his lips. "Ja, I am ready."

And she was. Ready for whatever the future had in store for them—together.

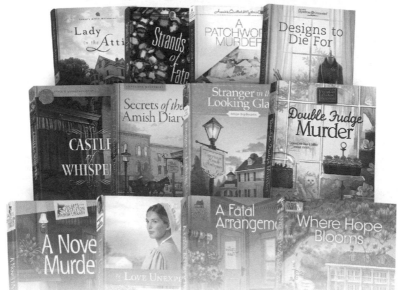